Henrietta H. House

EA Bundy

Eleven-year-old Henrietta and her little dog hide in a metal storage shed in the backyard to try and avoid the hexes her mother places on them. But that changes when Henrietta is given a talisman and made to hide it. She is to tell no one about it—ever! Despite her denials that she is a witch, just like her mother, the evil coven members are out to recruit her at any cost.

Henrietta H. House is a work of fiction. The characters, places of residence, and the incidents depicted are all products of the author's imagination and real place names are used fictitiously. They are not to be construed as portraying real events. Any resemblance to actual persons living or dead is purely coincidental.

~Singing Winds Press~
P.O. Box 131, Dallas, Oregon 97338
(Singing Winds Press is closed to submissions)

Library of Congress Control Number: 2012902149

Paperback ISBN: 978-1-61955-002-5
Electronic ISBN: 978-1-61955-003-2

DEDICATION

For readers of contemporary fantasy everywhere, but particularly
to those youthful readers who struggle with problems bigger
than most of us can comprehend. And especially to those in
public schools who have helped me to understand the challenges
they face. Their struggles and emerging wisdom helped me shape
Henrietta's life. May this story aid each one to escape
sometimes harsh realities and to contact their
own inner strengths, just as the main
character does in this story.

To my grandfather, KDB, who made each of us believe we were
his favorite, and to my brother, also KDB, who loves a good
story, and my mother, who sang as I lay in bed as a child,
making the world a safe place, a place where there
really can be happily ever after endings.
And to my daughter, with joy.

EAB

~Singing Winds Press~

Dallas, Oregon
Printed in the USA

CONTENTS

ACKNOWLEDGMENTS

My first reader, Noël, was as helpful and insightful as always.

My critique group members, Marian, Andrea, Charlie and Timothy were painstaking readers as well.

Jonathan's technological support was ongoing.

And I must not forget to mention Chris.

Hopefully, I didn't leave anyone out.

A big thanks to SWP for being there at just the right time.

1: HOW IT BEGAN

When the mother of Henrietta H. House screeched at her, the sound echoed through their unkempt home, continued out into the untidy yard, and reverberated through their otherwise ordinary neighborhood in Monmouth, Oregon. However, Mrs. House did not scream her daughter's *full* first name, but called her by the nickname *Henrie*.

So loudly did Henrietta's mother yell, the neighbors surely heard inside their homes. It was an astonishing noise made by an extraordinary woman.

"Henrieeeee!!!!"

That sound most definitely penetrated the metal tool shed in the backyard where Henrietta lay snuggled next to her little dog, a feisty Scottish terrier. They often huddled there together, hidden in a bed of straw amongst rusty rakes and shovels, and a smelly wheelbarrow.

In her mind, Henrietta only pretended to whisper, *Coming, mother*. That was because, with the assembled wisdom of all her eleven years, she had no intention of going into the messy house where her mom undoubtedly sat in her ancient, overstuffed chair.

Their home was one of those craftsman cottages constructed back in the 1920s over the remains of an even older structure. Built with a tall, secondary gable roof covering the entrance like a giant capital letter A, the overall blend of brick and woodwork, plus ornate leaded-glass windows was reminiscent of bygone eras. Although it had seen better days, the house was still interesting to look at. But from the street, one had to peer above a rusty, ornate gate in the overgrown hedge to catch a good glimpse of the mostly-hidden dwelling.

The small metal shed out back was Henrietta's refuge. Her dog, Elgin, was generally the only one who could find her there. He was named for a wristwatch he'd chewed up when he was a little puppy.

In his mistress' absence during school days, this shed was Elgin's hideout, since he could squeeze through the gap from a loose steel panel in the back wall. And although he was allowed to enter the home by himself through the pet door, he didn't unless Henrietta was home, because her mother had put one too many *hexes* on the lovable little pooch.

You see, Delvettica House was a self-proclaimed witch. Sixth generation, to be exact—as she so often bragged to her daughter—noting that Henrietta was a seventh generation witch girl.

A truly promising offspring, Henrietta even had the legendary nose like her mother's. One of those gosh-awful, long affairs, *not* the cute little turned-up sort that most girls had.

Except, unlike her mother, Henrietta's nose did not have an unsightly wart out near the end. For that, she was thankful, but her mom said it was only a matter of time before Henrietta had her own hideous growth. Delvettica, it seems, was also wart-free as a child. At least, that is what she said.

Henrietta shifted uncomfortably in her straw bedding left over from mulching the herb garden. Her nose wrinkled as she felt the signs that her mother was formulating a particularly nasty incantation to draw her only child inside the house to do her bidding. Elgin felt it too and whined, placing a paw over his snout.

As she sighed, and grudgingly whispered aloud, "Coming, mother," Henrietta subconsciously intensified those words without even trying.

Her mother's unfolding spell dissolved, although not for the reason Henrietta thought. She believed her mom's unnaturally acute hearing caught the whisper, causing her to withdraw the summoning hex. Not so.

Regardless of the fact that Henrietta rejected and fought against it, she was undoubtedly the most powerful young witch of her day, perhaps of all time. Despite her denial and resolve never to use such powers, that only magnified them, plus they manifested anyway, without her awareness.

With a sigh, Henrietta uncurled herself from Elgin and threaded her way through a maze of yard tools to the sliding door she'd left open just a crack. The metal shrilled as she slid the entry panel open. There was Elgin, already wagging his tail, awaiting her after having wiggled his way out through the metal flap at the rear of the structure.

Henrietta walked through the back door of her house and Elgin followed, toenails clicking on the tiles as if for moral support. A mixture of overpowering herb aromas, both rare and common, assaulted their noses. The plants hung from the kitchen ceiling to dry, casting ominous shadows across the floor and one wall. Elgin growled and his hair ruffled around his neck as he showed his teeth to the large black cat strolling by.

Henrietta called her mother's "pet" Sylvester, but her mom's name for the unusually large feline was Bast, after the Egyptian god with a cat's head. Elgin bristled whenever he encountered his nemesis, which had clawed him on numerous occasions.

In the barely-lit living room, Henrietta found her demanding parent sitting in the old chair just as she had imagined, except her mother was analyzing something cradled in her lap. Thus absorbed, the witch-woman seemed not to notice the presence of her daughter.

"Yes, Mum," Henrietta said, sounding as though she were from England, not the United States. It was a pretense she'd adopted long ago as a way of coping with her pitifully drab and isolated existence. But, as usual, her mother did not respond.

Henrietta stood there patiently. She was tall for her age, and her ungainly form seemed from another era or some part of the world untouched by modernization. She was one of those persons who invariably manage to look uncomfortable in their own bodies. The mismatched, out-of-date attire she wore did not help matters. It was comprised of ill-fitting, second-hand clothing her mother had deviously selected from a local thrift store.

Elgin sat beside his mistress with one paw on her foot, and leaned his head against her jeans. Henrietta wore boys' pants—mind you—not tastefully cut girls' jeans, and certainly not Capri pants. No. Just old baggy boys' dungarees, which were a source of much unnecessary teasing by other girls. Henrietta's mother said this would build witchly character, and that it was a family tradition handed down from previous generations.

Right, Henrietta thought. To her, it would be preferable looking the part of a "fashionable witch." That is, if she really was a witch—and she *wasn't*.

Henrietta was in denial about her witch-hood, and many other things. But who wouldn't be?

Her left foot tapped impatiently, clad in a worn-out tennis shoe. Not Conservator or any other name brand, but some imported poser no one ever heard of—and they were badly-worn, second-hand footwear at that. She continued tapping her foot. A girl could stand there only so long.

Her mother's eyes rose, looking toward Henrietta, but clearly her mom's mind was elsewhere because that gaze went right through her daughter. One gnarled hand shifted in her lap, revealing an old-fashioned, wooden clothespin lying there. The kind customarily made of two pieces of oak fastened together with a steel spring. It was the same type her mother used when securing herb bundles to strings that crisscrossed their kitchen ceiling. In modern American households, however, it was relegated to the long ago past.

This *particular* wooden pin had been carved upon, but Henrietta could not see what the woodworker had so carefully designed.

Absently, still staring beyond her daughter, Delvettica said, "Henrie, take this...hide it someplace even I can't find it, and tell no one about it—*ever!*"

She held the wooden clothespin out to her daughter.

2: NOT AS THEY SEEM

That word "ever," the way her mother had said it, probably meant *forever*. At least a lifetime. Henrietta examined the clothespin minutely. It was not oak like the others her mother used, but possibly black walnut, similar to their old-fashioned cutting board. The wood grain was rich, and varied in color from a pale tan, to cinnamon brown, plus a dark, chocolatey, almost-black shade.

A master carver had etched tiny figures across the surface, artistically combining them with the pattern of the wood grain. For some reason, Henrietta could not focus on the carvings because they made her mind go fuzzy.

She naturally cupped her hands around the heirloom in a protective fashion. Down at her feet, Elgin whined and danced about on the floor.

Meanwhile, Henrietta's hands felt warmth emanating from the wooden talisman. That word, *talisman,* popped into her mind, and seemed to fit the object. Her fingers squeezed in response to the warmth, and the heat intensified. However, before the temperature reached the burning point, it leveled-off.

Henrietta felt as if an inner fire had been kindled. Pleasant "flames" broadcast throughout her body, creating warmth that she would especially welcome on a blustery winter's day out in the metal shed.

Glancing at her mother, Henrietta saw the old witch had fallen into a deep daydream of some sort. Therefore, Henrietta quietly withdrew, thinking it better to leave while she could.

Passing along the hall and kitchen with some speed, she continued out to the backyard where she paused. There was a strong feeling she should not return to the shed for now. Where could she hide this talisman, and what significance did it hold for her mother?

With sudden inspiration, Henrietta returned to the kitchen. Elgin followed reluctantly, still whining. What was his problem? She found the ball of coarse string her mother used to suspend herb bundles from the ceiling. Henrietta cut off a double-arms-length piece with the utility scissors. In her mind's eye, she had seen herself wearing the talisman around her neck.

Forming a large loop in the string, Henrietta tied it off. Then she trimmed back the overly-long ends and slipped the circle around her neck, where it sagged into an oval. She clipped the wooden pin onto the knot at the bottom of the loop, and dropped it down through the neck opening in her shirt. The string was scratchy, but so were most of her clothes, and she'd learned to ignore such nuisances. The talisman settled reassuringly against her midriff.

Henrietta smiled for some unknown reason—she just couldn't help herself—and returned to the backyard, crossing to the alley gate. She was a block away before she realized that Elgin's whining behind her had turned to howls and frantic barks. She must have locked him in the yard. Probably just as well, without his leash.

Walking aimlessly south along Broad Street, she turned left away from the university campus. Henrietta kept straight on to the east, and without realizing it, drew ever nearer to her school. So distracted were her thoughts that her first hint about her location occurred when she heard shrill laughter coming from the playground equipment.

She decided to continue in that direction—something she would not ordinarily have done. Henrietta avoided other children as a rule because everything about her seemed to be part of a deliberate plan by her mother to cause peers to dislike her. The clothes she wore, for instance, and the disgusting smell of herbs that lingered about her.

Even her name, shortened to Henrie, aggravated other kids since it was so obviously a boy's. Also, there were weird occurrences that seemed always to surround Henrietta. Last and most significant was her strange mother, and the rumors of her being a witch. Unfortunately, these were true, and only scratched the surface of Henrietta's crazy reality.

As if that were not enough, Henrietta had added the made-up English accent—a deceit other kids detested. It was her way of trying to take charge of a situation entirely out of her control. She'd started that the year her mother insisted she be held back a grade.

Even if she could not make kids like her, she could make them dislike her, since she *really didn't care.* In that way, she gained some power over her impossible life. Taken together, these were enough to scare off any potential friends.

Her mother had forced Henrietta to read a book about two Jewish boys who were rivals at first, and then became friends. One was reared in a family tradition of silence other children did not understand.

"But we aren't Jewish!" Henrietta complained to her mother, and added in her mind that she also *was not* a boy.

Her mother had just nodded her head knowingly, as if agreeing with herself about something mysterious, and walked away carrying a dark secret she would not share.

As Henrietta approached the school swings, she saw two girls playing, and one looked up. For some reason, Henrietta did not cringe inwardly, as usual, but met the other's eyes with a smile and a "Hello." She uttered that greeting without her usual English accent.

"Hi," replied the blond girl. "Are you new here? Gonna come to this school?"

Henrietta recognized Allie, the most influential girl in her class. Why didn't Allie know her?

"Uh...yes." What else could Henrietta say, other than, *wake up and recognize one of your classroom nerds.* The second girl turned out to be Allie's best friend, Janna. The talisman under Henrietta's shirt hummed, and a surge of heat engulfed her body.

In moments, the three girls were playing gleefully, something Henrietta had *never* experienced before—despite the fact she'd observed others playing together on a daily basis. After climbing up the swing support posts, they chased each other around the play structure, weaving through the dangling chains until they all collapsed out-of-breath on their chosen seats.

Henrietta thought she would no longer beg her mother to let her be homeschooled, not that her mother ever would. Henrietta had pleaded for years, but her mother had simply cackled, "Public school builds witchly character."

Allie said to Henrietta, "You have the most beautiful, raven black hair."

Henrietta was stunned. No one had ever said anything like that to her before. "I do?"

"Yes," both of the girls agreed, their heads bobbing in unison. Unfortunately, a car horn honked just then, and a woman yelled out the window, "Allie, time to come home, dear."

"Bye, Henrietta," Allison yelled as she and Janna raced away. "See you at school tomorrow."

Henrietta continued to swing after they left, a smile lingering on her face. "They called me *Henrietta*."

She'd introduced herself by that name, not understanding why they didn't recognize her and call her Henrie. Whatever was going on was fine, if only this magical change would continue.

With the thought about *magical change*, Henrietta's hand went to her shirt where she felt the talisman. It was not humming as before, but rested there reassuringly under her clothing.

Walking the long way back home, she wondered what Monday at school would be like. There was hope in her heart for the first time. This was the only Sunday during the school year when Henrietta was not filled with dread from thinking about returning to her class.

She smiled and patted her talisman.

3: WHAT'S GOING ON?

The slight chill of spring air could not penetrate Henrietta's happy feelings. She smiled with delight. For the first time in her life, the hope she'd been afraid to even dream about actually seemed a possibility. She might be able to have friends.

The three main barriers to such a hope had moved to the back of her mind. She did not think about her mother casting the shadow of witchcraft across both their lives. Similarly, Henrietta did not worry about the way she looked, especially the length of her nose, and wearing Raggedy Anne's clothing. She'd also quit worrying for the moment about having an herbal odor.

Most significant of all, Henrietta did not have to push away her deepest, darkest secret. The fact that she had no father. Well, she had obviously been fathered, or she would not be alive, but she did not know who the man was. Her mother had never revealed his identity. The embarrassment of being fatherless had stung ever since Henrietta was old enough to realize it.

Never having a caring man in her life, not even a stepfather or uncle, Henrietta had sought out Mr. Baxter, the only male teacher in her school.

She'd volunteered to help around his classroom, cleaning and organizing after the last bell rang, even though she was not his student. Surprisingly, he had welcomed her assistance. He also accepted her just the way she was—all gangly, awkward, and smelling of herbs. For a little while, she had not felt repulsive, nor endured the stinging rejection of having no father.

Once Delvettica saw the change in her daughter, and realized where Henrietta spent so much of her time, Mr. Baxter became her target. He developed a nervous tic. At first, his left eye winked grotesquely at odd moments, and then it spasmed shut altogether. Next—young man though he was—he became inflicted with gout and hobbled around with a cane. Finally, he was forced into disability retirement, totally crippled by rheumatoid arthritis at the age of 23.

After that experience, and even though Henrietta tried to tell herself there really was no such thing as witchcraft—and that her mother could not possibly be a real witch—she avoided contact with men more than ever. When nice old Mr. Salido, who lived just down the street, began smiling and waving whenever Henrietta passed his yard as he worked in his garden, she quit walking anywhere near his house.

For the time being, however, Henrietta tried evading all such past negative thoughts and memories as she walked back toward her home from the playground.

The closer she came, however, the more that doubts and fears assailed her. Those two girls, Allie and Janna, would undoubtedly scream and run away when they saw Henrietta at school tomorrow. The attention they'd paid to her was probably just a deceit on their part. They would undoubtedly gather all her classmates around them at school to giggle and point at her.

The talisman hummed and generated heat that flowed through Henrietta like a soothing balm, quieting her hurtful thoughts, slowing her breathing rate, and calming her spirit.

When she eventually reached her front gate in the overgrown hedge at her house, Henrietta stopped. There was no frantic barking from Elgin, who simply sat on the weathered walkway behind the barrier. He did not race frantically about as was his usual manner of greeting. Instead, his black eyes studied her expectantly, waiting.

She pushed through the groaning entrance, assuming her mother's scream would fill her ears at any moment. The silence continued until she closed the gate, and its creaking protest shattered the quiet.

Henrietta walked cautiously around her home to the rear entrance because she *never* entered at the front of her house. Elgin followed on her heels, not racing ahead or leaping about. She opened the back door and pushed her head in, but there was no "welcoming" screech. Not even a harsh, "Henrietta, get your worthless little buttocks in here!"

Elgin's toenails pinged softly behind, as his mistress crossed the tiles. The only other sound was a strange droning one.

Peeking into the living room from the hallway, Henrietta saw her mother doing something she'd never observed before. Delvettica's head lulled to one side as she snored—sound asleep. That was the source of the droning noise.

Henrietta had come to believe her mother never slept. She'd not viewed her witchly parent in a non-conscious state before—ever. The woman looked absolutely peaceful. Even her age-lines had softened. For just a moment, Henrietta imagined her mother as a little girl, and pictured her as a child *not* filled with wickedness.

Delvettica's cat, Sylvester, crouched in the far corner, eyes gleaming with fear as she stared fixedly at the witch sleeping in the ancient chair. By contrast, Elgin neared the old woman without his usual fright, no longer hiding behind the security of his mistress.

Even when Henrietta drew near, her mother continued to doze peacefully, and the usually cruel look on her face was gone. Henrietta reached out in wonder to touch her mother's arm, then thought better of it, and retreated back the way she had come.

She'd never before realized how much she missed having a *real* mother.

In the hallway to the kitchen, she opened the upstairs door and climbed the steep steps. Elgin remained at the foot of the stairs, his head tilted quizzically to the side. He could not understand what she was doing. Henrietta never went up to her room anymore. Then he followed behind his mistress, his small feet bounding silently up the carpet runner that overlaid the hardwood treads.

Inside her musty bedroom, Henrietta paused. The black and white checkerboard pattern on the quilt covering her bed was just as she remembered seeing it last. The ornate spindles atop the dark wood bedposts seemed interesting. As she focused on them, she felt the talisman stirring feelings deep inside her, and the image of the wooden bedposts got clearer.

Henrietta imagined seeing them in their original elegance, long before they were the property of generations of witches, eventually becoming her mother's place to sleep, and finally, Henrietta's very own bed. Feeling suddenly drowsy, Henrietta lay on her black and white comforter—so much softer than the straw in the metal shed. The last things she remembered before sleep fully took her were the warmth of her talisman, Elgin snuggling at her side, and the hope she might actually have two new friends tomorrow.

4: AWAKE AT LAST

When Henrietta awoke, it was early morning. Her bedchamber was an assorted mixture of shadows cast by the first light of dawn's glow. Elgin snored softly on the quilt beside her, and Henrietta's unfocused eyes meandered around her room. Gradually, she noted areas of dull mist that were distinct from the black shadows she'd initially mistaken them for. Small clumps of darkish fog clung to certain objects in the room.

As her gaze fixed upon a shadowy vapor clinging to her plush bunny on the far wall's shelf, she held her breath, and concentrated. Her eyes focused clearly on the swirling haze of a thing seemingly alive. The layers of mist were then revealed to her, and at the same moment Henrietta heard her mother cackling at a great distance, or perhaps from an earlier time.

Henrietta re-experienced the long ago painful thoughts from holding her stuffed animal. Waves of sadness exploded within her as she heard her mother whispering in her mind's ear, generating feelings of loss at never having known her father. Henrietta had flung her bunny across the room with disgust and then placed it on the shelf, barely able to contain her impulse to throw it in the trash.

In her current moment of awareness, she knew the dark fogs distributed throughout her room were black spells cast by her mother. The realization scared Henrietta. When the sickening fears about witchcraft threatened to overwhelm her, the talisman beneath her shirt hummed, and warmth quickened in her body.

A pale glow kindled around Henrietta's bunny across the room. The dark mists surrounding her toy wiggled slowly, struggling against the growing power of the light, then became still, and dissolved away into nothing. The pain of loss previously associated with her toy disappeared, replaced by joy.

Henrietta identified another dull fog clinging to a doll on that same shelf. She heard the witchly cackle, and felt the suffering connected with her doll. It was an agony that through many spells had become her only feeling about her doll.

The warmth of her talisman and a flash of light caused the awful curses to be removed. The mist disappeared and in its absence fond memories returned to her of playing with her very first doll.

With ever-increasing speed, Henrietta glanced at objects in her bedroom that were cloaked in deadly spells, and set them free. In a few minutes, she lay peacefully beside her loyal dog, allowing a great sigh of relief to escape from her narrow chest. Her room was once again her refuge.

No longer would she and Elgin have to skulk about, or sleep in the old metal shed. However, she noticed a nagging itch on her right arm where it touched Elgin's coarse black hair. With a sudden apprehension, she sat up and stared at her dog.

He was totally encased by a tightly-layered cluster of dark spells. Why hadn't she noticed that before? With tears in her eyes, she recalled how he whined every time she left him at home and how he hid behind her whenever they entered the house.

The clothespin talisman vibrated at her solar plexus and light streamed forth, surrounding the small terrier. In moments, the shadowy mass fell away from her dog and disappeared. Her Scotty breathed more peacefully even though a small growl and bark escaped his mouth, and his feet twitched during some dream.

On impulse, Henrietta rose from bed and walked to the center of her room. Daylight had now filled the bedchamber with a honeyed-glow. Once again, her room was a safe haven, except for one extremely important detail she'd overlooked. Try as she might, she could not force herself to gaze into the full-length mirror attached to the closet door.

At last, Henrietta mustered all her courage and peered at her image. She nearly screamed. A thick cocoon of dark mists surrounded her body. Her face in the mirror peeked dimly back at her, as if through a grimy film.

Henrietta's talisman churned loudly and heat filled her, briefly bathing her lungs and insides with light. Then the living fire moved outward, pulsing in waves, like powerful X-rays, to engulf the dark spells that clung to her. The collection of hexes swelled like a dark wizard's cloak in a fierce wind, but finally dissolved, releasing its hold on her thin body.

In her mind's eye, she saw her mother writhing and moaning on the floor below, as many layers of witchcraft dissolved from her only child. In an agonized scream, the old witch relinquished the final remains of black magic used against Henrietta.

The looking glass image appeared to burst into light, shining through Henrietta's bedroom like a small but powerful sun. Before the freed eleven-year-old collapsed onto the floor, her mind registered the likeness of her transformed face. Instead of her former long nose Henrietta now had a more feminine one, although it was still not petite.

A smile of relief played upon her face as she slumped to the floor unconscious.

5: A NEW BEGINNING

When Henrietta awoke some time later, she found her braided throw rug had left impressions on her cheek. Elgin lay curled beside her, anxiously watching her face.

Glancing about her room, she noticed the sun had risen so that it broadcast a rectangle of light on her floor. Henrietta placed her arm around Elgin, drawing him even closer. Her bed chamber's lamp was off, yet the room glowed brightly. Way more than just what came from the sun through her window. As she looked closer, it seemed that all the objects in her bedroom had their own inner radiance. That was especially true of her bed. Henrietta stood up, hefting her loyal pet—so much heavier than he looked—and surveyed her surroundings.

The talisman hummed and the room brightened even more, as if a dimmer-switch had been turned to the highest setting. She squinted at first, but then she accustomed to the brilliance, and looked in the mirror. There stood a lovely girl with glistening, long black hair. Instead of her clothing looking dowdy, it appeared merely retro.

Curiosity caused Henrietta to move toward her bedroom's entrance, and as she went nearer, the door swung open automatically. She thought she heard faint trumpets in the background as she passed through the entrance-way. Once she exited, the overpowering light in her room automatically dimmed behind her. The stairway before Henrietta brightened as she descended down it, and as she entered the lower hallway, the stairway darkened behind her.

In the living room, she discovered her mother's body sprawled out on the floor. The twisted face seemed frozen in a silent scream. When Henrietta leaned nearer, however, she heard the soft rattle of breath that indicated her mother still lived.

Elgin growled deep in his throat, and struggled so greatly, he freed himself from his mistress' arms and plunged to the floor. His small feet scrambled briefly to regain balance, and then he raced toward the corner where a dark shape crouched in fear. Before he reached Sylvester, the old witch's cat ran for her life down the hallway to the kitchen. Elgin's feet scrabbled after her on the slippery tiles. There was a repetitive smashing sound as the large feline banged into the back door, and then switched to the pet entrance, which allowed her to escape.

Elgin returned to the living room, his steps high and brisk, his short tail waving jauntily in the air. He went right up to the prostate form and growled again.

"Elgin," Henrietta said. "She might be hurt."

Her Scottish terrier turned his back and walked off as if to say, So!

Something told Henrietta that her mother would likely recover and there was nothing more to be done for that moment.

An alarm clock blasted from down the hall—a horrendous sound.

"It's time to get ready for school!" Henrietta shouted, and raced to the stairway to silence the deafening buzzer; but no sooner did she think of turning it off, than it ceased.

6: HER "NEW" SCHOOL

Singing as she showered and dressed, Henrietta actually looked at her clothing when she put it on. She carefully matched the colors and textures until she was satisfied. Looking in the mirror, she barely recognized herself. Although she was not clothed as a contemporary girl of Monmouth, she had managed an acceptable appearance.

Walking down the sidewalk just before she arrived at school, she worried that Allie and Janna would not recognize her, but such concerns vanished as she heard a familiar voice.

"Henrietta," a girl called to her from a little way behind and across the street. "We're over here."

Sure enough, as Henrietta looked in their direction, she recognized the girls she'd played with the day before. "Hi Allie...Janna."

The other two raced to join her, and their presence caused the rest of her surroundings to become a blur as Henrietta talked with her new friends.

"You'll probably be in my class," Allie said. "We have less kids, and that's how they decide where to put new students."

Henrietta had not thought about this. Surely the teacher or someone would recognize her, and if they did not, what would they do about the missing Henrie?

None of those concerns turned out to be of consequence as Henrietta eventually found herself in Mrs. Persimmons' class seated right behind Allie. Henrietta's nearly-empty backpack rested on her desk. She was treated matter-of-factly by the teacher, and adored by the other students, particularly the girls, who all wanted her to sit by them at lunch. No one seemed to notice when Henrietta occasionally got up and retrieved things from Henrie's desk, placing them in her new location.

The school day was half over when Henrietta observed that every time the teacher turned her back to the class, she did so with great speed, and a strange shadow briefly appeared like a double image. It was as if something were trying to hide while clinging to Mrs. Persimmon. When Henrietta focused more on this puzzle, she felt warmth at her midriff.

Thank goodness she had remembered to put the good luck amulet back around her neck. There was a flash of light that the others did not seem to notice, and a high-pitched screech as the shadowy form dropped to the floor and disappeared in a puff of dust. No one else observed that, either.

On the way home after school, Henrietta walked partway with her two new best friends.

"Can you come over to my house," Allie asked. "My mom wants to meet you, and Janna's mom is allowing her to come over."

Janna nodded agreement, looking expectantly at Henrietta.

"Uh, I'd have to ask my..."

Janna pulled out her cell phone. "Just call and say we need to do homework together. Later, we'll ask if you can stay for dinner."

Henrietta felt like she had died and gone to heaven, but said, "I can't, guys...mom's sick, and I got to get home fast. Maybe tomorrow?"

The other girls were disappointed, but Allie looked thoughtful and added. "If your mom's better by then, you can come over and have dinner with us."

Janna hopped up and down with enthusiasm. "Oh yes, that would be *so cool.*"

Henrietta reluctantly left her friends and continued homeward.

When she passed through the wrought iron front gate, it squealed in protest as it typically did, but for the first time she noticed something else. Although she had gone through it on innumerable occasions, in this instance she recognized symbols interspersed with the simple decorative flutes. They were symbols associated with the black magic pentagram, a five-pointed star designed inside a circle. Like the one her mother had painted on the floor of her spell-casting room.

Elgin, tail wagging, awaited Henrietta to follow her into the house. For the first time she could remember, they went through the *front* door. Elgin was initially reluctant, but then he trotted ahead of her to the parlor entrance outside the living room. For a second, Henrietta paused, worry filling her mind with what was about to greet her inside that room.

7: HOUSE TO HOME

Delvettica House sat in her customary chair, her head tilted toward the floor, eyes open wide but unfocused, as though she were lost in reverie. She did not appear to notice Henrietta's presence. Moving nearer, Henrietta saw that her mother's face seemed ten years younger. How odd.

Looking around the living room, Henrietta noted the dark and dismal coating that had gradually accumulated on the surface of everything over the years. Impulsively, she went to the window and pulled open the massive drapes. Light streamed in and when Henrietta turned around, she saw the dark shadows, which were really disembodied shapes that appeared nearly everywhere. They tried to shrink in size in an unsuccessful attempt to evade detection.

Henrietta thought about how long she had denied these facts about her mother. She'd tried to believe witchcraft was a sham, simply the deluded and misguided rumblings of an eccentric old woman. Now, the reality "glared" at her from every nook and corner.

She had tried unsuccessfully to hide in the tool shed to get away from this awful truth. Without the amulet, she would still be hiding out, the victim of this horrid creature whom she called mother, and now sat across the room in that ancient chair.

Delvettica had not moved and continued in her trance-like state even as Henrietta purposefully reached to her middle and grasped the talisman beneath her fabric top. Light seemed to explode outward in all directions, targeting each misty form, dissolving them simultaneously—accompanied by loud wailing.

Henrietta sighed with satisfaction. She was getting pretty good at this spell removal business. Strange that her mother did not notice what was going on around her. Henrietta pulled absently on the string around her neck and withdrew the talisman, studying it.

She was now able to focus on the tiny carvings, which were reminiscent of scrimshaw work she'd seen at the Jensen Arctic Museum west of the campus. Except, this engraving was done on hardwood instead of ivory. She squinted closer, and detected a row of small human figures holding hands as they curved around the surfaces of the clothespin amulet.

The last shape in the formation was smaller and brighter than the others, resembling a star with rays of light shooting out in carved lines. Henrietta didn't know why she felt shaky inside, and her eyes misted over, almost forcing her to put the amulet away.

Looking again at her mother, Henrietta noticed a dark cloud above Delvettica's head, and as she moved nearer, she saw something like a miniature diorama inside the cloud. It reminded her of one of those glass ball paperweights that you can shake up and down to watch a snowy scene. Only this was a dark and murky world within the little cloud.

As she watched the images, she identified a baby in its cradle set in the middle of the big pentagram in her mother's hexing room—except this version was much smaller. Something about the dingy setting made Henrietta want to turn away, but she could not.

She also heard a dismal voice and glimpsed the moving shadow of a person, plus a ceremonial knife raised above the baby, its point tipped with blood so dark it seemed black—slowly dripping.

Henrietta tried, but could not close her eyes. A second, softly-spoken female voice explained the meaning of the unfolding drama. "In black magic, the greatest power comes from sacrificing innocent blood. A helpless baby is the most innocent of all."

Henrietta shuddered and squeezed her clothespin amulet tightly as she heard the baby's cry. The talisman turned white hot and a scorching light as brilliant as a thunderbolt, flashed into the dark world swirling above her mother's head, shattering the images. Delvettica screamed as if she had been stabbed by the dripping knife. Yet, she did not come out of her trance. But after the scream, Henrietta's mother seemed more peaceful than ever.

Browsing the room with her eyes, Henrietta discovered all trace of the shadowy forms and darkness had been removed.

A noise attracted her attention and Henrietta swiveled to look downward. There she saw Elgin wiggling with anticipation while staring up at Henrietta's mother, and then he jumped onto the woman's lap. Delvettica's hand went automatically to the Scotty dog's neck, stroking his black hair.

Henrietta had never seen such behavior; her mother had always been mean to the small terrier. When her pet returned to the floor, Henrietta's mother remained in her sleep-like state.

Elgin followed his mistress into the kitchen and sat attentively at her feet as she surveyed the cooking environment. Delvettica had not cooked in ages. All that Henrietta ate in recent years came from one box or another out of the cupboard. Or from the small freezer above the old refrigerator, to be microwaved into an edible, if tasteless state.

Henrietta's gaze was drawn to a particular knife in the wooden knife rack. The blade resembled a dagger and reminded her of the one she'd seen in the blackened image above her mother's head. A hateful darkness thicker than any she'd noticed before surrounded this blade in the kitchen.

It felt to her as though a vicious presence had possessed this piece of cutlery. Henrietta's upper body shivered as she recalled it was undoubtedly the same knife that she had sliced herself with whenever her mother forced her to chop up herbs.

Old fears of being cut started to overwhelm Henrietta, but she still gripped her talisman and it hummed to life, raising a globe of illumination around her hand. The sphere of light increased its intensity and rose into the air, floating swiftly to the knife rack and surrounding the offensive blade.

The fierce burning that resulted went on for several minutes, and when it finally stopped, the offending knife was twisted and distorted almost beyond recognition. It certainly could not be withdrawn from its rack.

For the first time after one of these spell reversals, Henrietta felt drained. She stumbled down the hall and up the stairs where she fell into bed, with Elgin turning round and round beside her before curling into a ball.

8: RESTLESS SLEEP

Henrietta slept fitfully during the night, partly waking at times. During such alert moments, she forced herself back into her world of dreams, not wanting to face the real-life yuckiness smothering her restless slumber.

When the clock blared at last, her dream world was shattered, but splinters of it clung in her memory as she sat up. Why was she still haunted by fears when she had dissolved so many wicked spells in her life?

She'd not had this much trouble sleeping out in the shed, even with her makeshift mattress. There, she wasn't aware of her dreams, if she dreamed at all. What did last night's ordeal mean? Was something awful about to happen?

Henrietta forgot her problems of the night as she neared school. She tried not to think about her mother still sitting in her living room chair, not eating or drinking, and not really waking or sleeping.

As if it was all planned ahead, Henrietta met Allie and Janna where they had joined up the previous morning. This time, as they walked to school, Henrietta was more aware of what occurred around her.

"That little bee-atch Tabitha is going to get hers," Allie said.

Janna added, "Yeah, who does she think she is? The little poser...she's just a wannabe."

Henrietta was shocked by their language and asked, "Who is Tabitha?"

"Yeah," Allison said. "Who is she?"

"She's nobody," Janna said.

Both girls laughed and then Allison explained that Tabitha was this *popular girl* in another fifth grade class. Only, the way she said "popular" made it sound like something awful, almost a death sentence.

"She used to be our friend," Janna said. "Until–"

Allison cut her off. "She invited us to her party."

That didn't sound like a reason to hate her, Henrietta thought.

"...her party with all the *nerds*," Janna added.

"Can you imagine?" Allison turned to her newest friend.

Henrietta shrugged, swallowed hard, and "No. Not really." Her mind was scrambling to understand. She'd never seen enough of other kids' friendships first-hand to know what they were really like. She thought she'd only missed out on one child getting to know another, and hanging out–but not this kind of pettiness.

Although Henrietta entered her "new" school in a daze, she was able to focus her talisman to remove two dark hexes clinging to the principal's door. How had she missed seeing those yesterday?

Once seated behind Allison in the classroom, Henrietta watched her new friends carry on a critical conversation about Tabitha that included whispered terms like "Ho," and others that made Henrietta blush. They soon outlined a strategy to make Tabitha late for class after recess. Their plot involved another kid in class, Cory, who along with the now absent Henrie did not have a single friend.

Nobody seemed to notice Henrie's absence, let alone miss her.

If ever a boy was a nerd, it was Cory. He carried his scientific calculator with him everywhere. The two girls were going to get friendly with him at recess and have him carry a verbal message from Allison to Tabitha. He would tell Tabitha to meet Allison in the girl's restroom. It was supposed to be "top secret," and *super important.* He was to tell Tabitha, "Don't leave until you talk to Allie."

Janna and Allie would make Cory rehearse it several times until he got it just right.

Because the message was not written, it would be easy to deny they'd said it. When Cory eventually got into trouble for making up stories—and the girls were convinced he would—who cared about him? He was, after all, just another nerd.

The tardy bell was often hard to hear in the girl's restroom, but just to be certain Tabitha was late, there was a second part to the plan. Adelle was second runner-up for top nerd status, and had irritable bowel syndrome. She could use the restroom whenever she wanted. Adelle would stay in there and continuously flush the toilet—a sound that would cover any hint of the warning bell.

The girls chuckled as they finished telling their devilish plan. For the moment, they seemed to have forgotten all about their new friend Henrietta, sitting just behind Allison.

Henrietta had to admit it seemed a fool proof scheme. Her next thought was to wonder how soon it would be before these two plotters decided she needed some "well-deserved" punishment? She was seriously considering that when another idea popped into her head.

Were these girls victims of witchcraft—or perhaps they were actually young witches in training? She knew they weren't eleven-year-old witches, since they would have been whispering evil spells instead of working out their current plan. But their minds seemed to be using the same basic principles of witchcraft—doing damage to those who were weak, vulnerable, or unaware.

Looking carefully at Janna as she was turned in profile, Henrietta could not see any sign of a dark mist clinging to her that would indicate she was the victim of sorcery.

Getting up to sharpen her pencil, although it was already sharp, Henrietta used that excuse to view both of her friends from a distance, to determine if they had any of the obvious signs of witchery. They did not.

In fact, after yesterday, the entire room was clear of any suspicious dark spots.

During recess, Allison and Janna were so intent on carrying out their treachery, they didn't seem to notice that Henrietta had drifted off to another area of the playground. She watched their unfolding mischief with growing alarm as Cory left them to deliver his little speech to Tabitha, who was halfway across the play yard.

So disturbed was Henrietta as she focused on Cory's progress, she wished he would have an accident along the way, preventing him from delivering his message. No sooner did the thought enter her mind than he tripped and fell, screaming loudly.

When a playground attendant helped Cory to hobble toward the building, Henrietta saw that a dark mist clung to his back. She shuddered. Had *she* done that to him? Although she did not want to admit the possibility, the fact was very evident. She had accidentally hexed and injured Cory. She hadn't really meant to, but that did not change the outcome. He was hurt, and it was her fault.

Henrietta thought she could hear a witch cackling in the distance. A shiver went up Henrietta's back, and she raced toward the school building, focusing her mind on her talisman as she ran. Her eyes were fixed on the dark spot on Cory's back when her amulet hummed, and a white light flashed. The offensive dark patch on his back dissolved.

Almost instantly, Cory stood erect, tested out his foot, and told the attendant he was fine. She looked puzzled, but stood and watched as he *ran* back to the playground to carry out his assigned task.

Henrietta turned away in disbelief. What was she to do? If she did nothing, Tabitha would get into trouble, but if she used witchcraft, she would be heading down that horrid life path, maybe for good, and eventually turning out like her mother.

9: PUZZLE TO ENIGMA

Should Henrietta try and intervene again? Or would she just stand by and watch this treachery unfold? She walked slowly toward the school, but had not gone far before she heard racing footsteps and looked to see Tabitha sprinting ahead of her toward the doorway. Henrietta started to yell out, but thought better of it. Allie and Janna would target her for sure if they knew she rescued Tabitha. Cory darted through the school door just moments after Tabitha entered. He was most likely making sure she went into the restroom.

Piercing laughter erupted farther out on the playground. Henrietta recognized Janna's shrill squeal, and turned to see Allie clinging to a swing, laughing so hard she could barely keep from falling over.

So occupied with their merriment were the two schemers, they would not notice if Henrietta went inside the school, and even if they did, they would not think her motive was to go and warn Tabitha. But before she could enter, the fire alarm rang. She stopped just paces from the entrance as three students exited in a hurry. One of the two boys was Cory, and the girl was Tabitha. A moment later, Adelle rushed from the school.

Great timing, Henrietta thought. I don't have to get involved now. Why didn't I think of setting off the alarm? Not that she would ever do that.

The obnoxious blaring of the bell continued and Henrietta joined the flow of students moving farther out in the play area where an attendant was organizing them into rows by classroom.

Besides the welcome diversion, and the undoing of the plan to harm Tabitha, it was a nice spring day for a fire drill. Henrietta moved toward the back of the line filled with her classmates. Passing Jana and Allie, she saw their heads huddled together as she walked unnoticed beyond them.

"No talking," said an adult, and the drone of voices lowered quite a bit.

"Face away from the school," said another woman, whose words were followed by the mumbling from students as they slowly complied with her direction.

One boy said loudly enough for many children to hear, "We want to watch it burn."

Gasps followed his remark, and a temporary silence came just before the distant blasting of the fire department's siren. The student's quiet deepened and then fearful whispers were heard. "Maybe the school really is on fire."

Henrietta noticed Tabitha standing in the nearby line on her left, just ahead of her, talking to a girl from the other class as more teachers arrived to help organize and quiet their students.

From a few blocks away came the mixture of siren sounds and occasional loud honking that meant emergency vehicles were approaching the school.

"There goes recess," whispered a boy two kids ahead of Henrietta, and she realized it was Cory.

Upset whispers followed his remark, and then total silence as emergency vehicles arrived at the school and pulled into the parking lot out front. Henrietta could not help but turn her head to watch, seeing the cab of a fire truck with its lights flashing brightly.

The other students stared as well, along with the teachers. This was obviously not a drill. The girl in the line beside Henrietta sobbed quietly, "What if our school does burn?"

The other students were not as worried, but the total silence remained, and upset looks covered all the faces Henrietta could see.

"Turn away from the school," said a teacher. "It is likely to be a false alarm, but the firemen must be certain and check the entire building."

Reluctantly, students followed her instruction. Having officials checking-out the building seemed to take forever. Minutes seemed like hours, and

Henrietta's mind wandered. Whatever had become of Mr. Baxter? The last she'd heard–

Strange to say, at that very moment, a conversation began in the line to Henrietta's right, interrupting her thoughts, and yet continuing them.

"He just lays in bed most of the time. Meals on Wheels comes to his house. Hardly anybody visits him, except Tabitha."

"Miss goody-two–"

"What?" Tabitha said from just past Henrietta, in the line on the other side.

The girls who had been talking paused awkwardly, and then one of them said, "Nothing...we were just talking about Mr. Baxter...how you go and see him."

"Poor old Mr. Baxter," said that girl's companion. "It's really sad...but nice of you to visit." They turned away from the direction of Tabitha and began whispering so softly that Henrietta could not hear what they said.

Tabitha scowled with suspicion at the pair, and then her eyes by chance locked with Henrietta's. Tabitha smiled. Henrietta automatically smiled back, and in that instant, she decided she liked Tabitha. She also decided she didn't like Allie and Janna, but a new idea entered her mind, and she asked Tabitha, "Could I come with you sometime when you visit Mr. Baxter?"

"Sure. I'm going over there after school today. Meet me out front."

"Thanks!"

The all-clear bell sounded a moment later and Henrietta realized the emergency vehicles, including an ambulance, were driving away. The students were filing back toward the school entrance in a long line, one class after the other.

Henrietta was glad that Allie and Janna had been too far away from her in their class queue to hear the conversation she'd had with Tabitha.

"I wonder who pulled the alarm?" a boy asked just behind Henrietta.

She turned in surprise to see Cory. How did he get there?

"What?" She asked.

He smiled and looked off in the direction where the last fire truck retreated. Then he added, "Alarms don't just pull themselves."

10: ENIGMA'S TWIST

After school, Henrietta waited out front for Tabitha. With each deep, fast breath, she feared Allie and Janna would appear, and wondered what she'd tell them. Feeling vulnerable—as if she was the last tree standing in a clear-cut—Henrietta waited nervously for her two "friends" to come and verbally chop her down. Which is what they would do when they discovered why she waited there, and realized she did not plan to go home with them. Maybe she should lie? She would, except she couldn't think of a good story to tell.

Henrietta recognized Allie's car driving slowly in front of the school, with Allie's mother at the wheel. The Mercedes slowed and two girls who had been half-hidden by a parked car leaped inside just before it drove away.

Were they looking back out the tinted rear window and laughing at Henrietta? Probably not. They likely had some appointment they needed to go to. Perhaps a Mean Girls, Inc. meeting, or something similar.

The dark automobile turned the corner and was lost from sight.

"Hi," a girl said from just behind Henrietta.

Henrietta was so surprised and shocked when she turned and saw who Tabitha's companion was that she simply stared.

"Ready...?" Tabitha asked, and added, "Cory goes with me sometimes. Do you know him?"

Henrietta nodded slowly. She was about to accompany Allie and Janna's Public Enemy Number One—namely Tabitha—along with the biggest nerd in school on a mission that was undoubtedly going to be her social undoing.

Henrie might as well return.

Walking down the street with her two companions, Henrietta realized she'd been *ditched* by her "best friends," Allie and Janna. If it hadn't been for that, they would have witnessed this act of social self-destruction on her part. Only one thing could make this moment even more complete, in the sense of total peer rejection. Henrietta had a suspicion she was about to enter into the Nerd Hall of Fame—for all time....

"Hey guys...wait up!"

Henrietta did not have to turn around to look. Even if she had not recognized the voice, she knew this could only be one person on earth.

Just perfect, she thought.

"Hi, Adelle," said Tabitha. "I thought you had to stay after school..."

Henrietta did not hear the rest of their small talk. She was wallowing in self-pity.

She found herself saying, "What?" as she was yanked back from her awful reverie. "What did you say?"

"How did you know Mr. Baxter," asked Adelle. "You weren't in his class."

It was a long story, the true details of which she did not care to disclose. "Uh, I used to help him after school...sometimes."

"Oh. We help too," said Adelle. "There's lots of things he can't do around his house."

Tabitha added, "Watering his plants. Changing his bedding...taking out the trash...we also answer his e-mails...pay his bills..."

"So," interjected Cory with a laugh, "who do you suppose pulled the fire alarm?"

"You and your rhetorical questions," said Tabitha. "Enough already. We're almost there."

"Rhe–what?" Henrietta asked. She was an avid reader when there was enough daylight to see inside the metal shed, since she'd had lots of free time in there and no TV. Her vocabulary was exceptional for her age, but that word had thrown her.

"It means he knew the answer before he asked us the question," Tabitha explained.

A large mastiff-crossbred dog crashed against the chain-link fence along the sidewalk, uttering a hair-raising, throaty growl that sent chills through Henrietta.

"Down, Duke," Tabitha commanded, paying the large canine almost no mind. "He's a pussycat, really... starved for attention. Sometimes we take him on walks for Mr. Baxter."

Henrietta had stopped when the guard dog interrupted them, now she noticed he stared at her, and tilted his head to the side, like he was curious about her. He whined as if he wanted out of the fence.

"He likes you," said Tabitha. "Likes you a lot. Maybe you should walk him."

The giant, brutish-looking head pressed against the fence, eyes begging.

Despite her initial fears, Henrietta found her hand touching the fence. Her fingers slipped inside the wires and stroked his muzzle.

"I'll go too," said Cory. "I don't usually get to walk the dog."

11: MR. BAXTER

Inside the modest house, Henrietta immediately noticed aromas that she associated with sick people and hospitals. There was also an underlying mustiness from lack of air circulation, which didn't help matters. She briefly longed for the herbal scents that permeated her own house. After a moment of imagining, she thought she could actually smell strong herbs in Mr. Baxter's home.

"Did somebody burn incense in here?" Cory asked.

Adelle said, "It does smell different."

"Lots better," agreed Tabitha.

The foursome went down a hallway from the front room and entered a bedroom. Henrietta was last to go inside. She barely stilled a groan as she viewed the twisted body on the bed. Mr. Baxter was but a very sad resemblance of his former self.

Impulsively—as the others gathered about the hospital bed that held their past teacher—Henrietta went to the window and adjusted the old Venetian blind to let in more light. She also lifted the shade up and opened his window.

The others who'd brought Henrietta into the house gasped at her actions.

She looked over and saw Mr. Baxter's right eye squinting in what appeared to be a painful way. She stepped closer to him, blocking the sunlight from his face. Even in the shadow she cast, she recognized that his left eye was almost entirely closed in a permanent spasm.

His brow was furrowed, and creases lined his forehead as though he were a man in his eighties, not his early twenties.

Tabitha moved toward the window as if to readjust the shade, but Mr. Baxter raised his right arm, and mumbled, "That's alright. Fresh air will do me good."

As the others talked excitedly with their former teacher, Henrietta did not really hear what they said. Her attention was fixed on Mr. Baxter's fingers, twisted by arthritis until they were almost useless—reminding her of the crooked legs of a crab. She could only imagine the pain he felt.

Then her eyes refocused on his body and she saw what would have been invisible in the darkened room. The man's form was enclosed by a black cocoon of flowing mists that swirled and eddied all around him.

Henrietta's right hand went automatically to the area of her amulet resting beneath her shirt. The fingers of her other hand reached out and touched the gnarled "claw" Mr. Baxter had raised—that was still suspended in the air.

She felt her amulet pulsing, and white hot energy surged through her body, down her arm and hand into Mr. Baxter's fingers. There was a slight shudder, and she noticed intense vibrations traveling under the surface of his skin. She likewise saw the black mists surrounding his torso writhe like a mass of snakes suddenly invaded by a king cobra that would soon eat them all.

Mr. Baxter took a deep breath and sighed. "I always feel so much better when you children visit me. Thanks for coming today."

Henrietta studied the man before her. His fingers had straightened slightly, or was that her imagination? His left eye appeared to be open wider than before, though still not back to normal. And the wrinkles in his forehead—made deep from constant pain—had softened as well.

She stepped to the side, allowing sunshine to reach Mr. Baxter. His right eye blinked, then seemed to clear.

He watched the youngsters as they scurried about doing their "duties," making the room tidy by picking up trash that had missed the garbage can. They helped him scoot to one side of the bed in preparation for changing his sheets.

"Come on," said Cory to Henrietta, "Let's walk Brutus."

Adelle corrected, "His name is Duke."

"Whatever," Cory replied, grabbing Henrietta's right arm—unaware that he was removing it from the area of her amulet—and pulled her from the room, guiding their way around to the back door.

12: WHO'S LEADING?

Taking the huge dog for a walk turned out to be even more of a task than Henrietta had imagined. Cory made Duke sit and stay while attaching the leash to his collar, and the big dog was cooperative until they led him out through the yard's side gate. From then on, it was all that the two of them could do to create enough drag on the leash to slow him down.

Less than a block from Mr. Baxter's home, Henrietta clung to Cory's belt, trying to slow his and Duke's progress. But the mastiff easily dragged them both, as if they wore inline-skates instead of shoes. Henrietta's worn-out sneaker soles skidded along the sidewalk no matter what she tried. She hoped they would not wear all the way through, allowing the pavement to dig into her feet.

When Duke turned the corner, he dragged the kids at an angle across the lawn. Cory went to his knees, and Henrietta lost her balance, dropping to the ground after releasing her grip on his belt.

As she tried to stand, Henrietta felt something cold on her neck, She discovered it was Duke's nose, and then his big wet tongue slobbered on her cheek. The dog sat there with a giant grin on his face, as if waiting for them to resume the pulling game. Cory laughed himself silly, rolling around on the ground. And then Henrietta put her arms around his big hairy neck–the dog's, not Cory's–and gave him a hug.

Duke rolled onto his side and Henrietta found herself sprawled half on top of him, arms still clinging to his neck. She laughed and wrestled the monster dog, who responded by placing a foreleg across her middle.

Henrietta heard the buzz of her talisman and felt warmth filling herself and the dog. In another minute, Duke was half asleep on the grass, with Henrietta's head on his chest.

Cory ceased his chuckling and moved closer to the pair, studying them with curiosity.

When Henrietta finally stood up, Duke watched her absently.

With a tug on his leash, she got the mastiff to stand. Then the three walked calmly on around the sidewalk.

"You sure have a way with dogs," Cory told Henrietta.

She nodded without comment. "How far do you usually take him?" she asked.

"Just one time around the block, but we could go farther today if you want."

"Okay." She had no idea what else to do to help Mr. Baxter. Tabitha and Adelle seemed to have everything else under control at the house. Henrietta asked, "What did you mean about the fire alarm...what you said earlier."

"I went along with Allie and her gremlin-gang partner," Cory said, "even though they hate me and I can't stand them. If I hadn't, they'd of found somebody else to do their dirty work. That way, I could mess with their plans."

Maybe Cory wasn't such a nerd after all, Henrietta decided.

"You seem to be their new best friend," he said.

"That's what I thought too, at first, but now I'm not so sure."

Duke walked happily between the two, not pulling on his leash. Henrietta rested her arm across his back and thought about her situation. Maybe not aligning with Allie and Janna was a better plan than she would have thought. It sure was weird, though, how friendly they had been to her at first.

"They suck-up to any new students for awhile," Cory said, "until they get a chance to *use* them. But when they got tired of their new play thing...that's when they really mess them over."

Henrietta thought about that, and guessed it was true. Probably they were already hatching plans aimed at her. Henrietta's cheeks felt flushed as she realized what a fool she'd been.

"Hang with Tabitha," Cory said. "She won't let you down. Anyone can be her friend...more kids like her than anybody else in school, and the Dragon Twins are just jealous. She invites them to her parties, but they never come–too stuck-up. Adelle and I are free agents. Don't let on to Allie and Janna that we have any friends, otherwise, we can't protect Tabitha."

Henrietta decided the friendship situations were definitely not what they had at first seemed to be.

13: THE DISCOVERY

Henrietta H. House walked home with much on her mind after her visit with Mr. Baxter. For some of the way a small smile lingered as she recalled her interactions with Duke. He was a truly lovable big dog.

None of her recent and unsettling friendship experiences, however, had prepared her for what she discovered when she walked through her own front gate at home. Elgin was not waiting expectantly as he had been for the last few days. Instead, he came reluctantly from his hiding place under the overgrown laurel hedge.

He did not run ahead to the front door, but whimpered and held back. When she started toward the porch, Elgin grabbed hold of her pant-leg with his teeth, snarling and attempting to hold her back.

Henrietta tried to shake him loose without hurting the Scotty, and finally reached down to pick him up. He shivered fearfully in her arms as she proceeded up the steps and over to the door. Her reassuring whispers had no effect on him, and as she managed to get the door open partway, she mysteriously found that she had a lump in her throat, making it hard to swallow.

A dull echo of arguing voices issued from within the house, causing her to halt with uncertainty. Shivers ran up and down her spine.

Elgin's hind legs scrambled, his claws hurting her arm, and his chunky body twisted so strongly that she was forced to release her hold. He flung himself to the porch floor and raced away around the house.

"Then, where is she?" a shrill voice asked above the soft din of murmurings beyond the entrance hall—probably from the living room.

A second, equally high-pitched tone brought silence within the house, "She's arrived at last...the *little dear.*"

There was nothing comforting in the way the woman said "little dear."

A strong and demanding feeling drew Henrietta inside her now-quiet home. Past the foyer's coat closet, the invisible force tugged her irresistibly onward. She paused in the receiving room just beyond, with its old-fashioned coat rack weighted down by black capes. Even the benches lining the walls were littered with dark robes. Henrietta did not want to enter the living room, but the unseen power compelled her onward against her will.

A strange, whispered question broke the stillness before she actually went in.

"Does she know...?"

"Shhhh."

Entering the living room, Henrietta found the window curtains were closed and the lights were turned off. The only illumination came from a row of candles on top of the fireplace mantle.

The room was full of dark forms.

"Here she is...here's our little witch girl."

Henrietta approached the center of the room as if riding on an invisible people mover. When she halted automatically beside her mother, who was still sitting in her chair, there was an invisible energy, like electromagnetism, that made Henrietta's hair want to stand on end.

"Let us have a look at you."

Strong fingers gripped Henrietta's elbow, forcing her body to turn. She saw the face of a tall witch who resembled her mother. The smell of an overwhelming incense filled the room, making it hard for Henrietta to breath.

She was pushed this way and that in the next few minutes, until she had been viewed from every possible direction by all the witches.

They uttered satisfied cackles of approval.

This must be the often-mentioned coven her mother had referred to. None of the faces were familiar, and yet they all had a sameness that was disconcerting—except for one witch who lacked the long hooked nose. Hers was a singularly attractive appearance, and yet there was something entirely wrong about it. Henrietta could not determine what that wrongness actually was, for she could not make herself study the witch's lovely face. A fearful premonition caused her to look away.

In fact, she found herself tilting her head so she could gaze at the ceiling instead of studying the witches. On the overhead surface, she discovered strange bumps she'd never noticed before. They were an exaggeration of the acoustical surface made ominous by the flickering light cast from the candles. Then she saw one of the seemingly architectural bulges move, and realized the forms scattered about up there were bats.

Gulping, Henrietta's eyes lowered to the witch standing just in front, and she could not help staring at the large wart on the side of her nose. Henrietta's breathing was more like gasping for air by that time. She had never been so scared as then, surrounded by a room full of witches, all equal in their cruelty to her mother—if not more so.

"Be a good little witch and go to your room."

That order came from the more attractive one, apparently their leader, though once again Henrietta discovered she could not study the face to discover what was not right about it.

Henrietta's body left the room almost of it's own will, and as she entered the hallway leading to the kitchen, she realized the "pretty" witch's features seemed real, and yet they were not. Those attractive physical traits were a projected mask. Henrietta's breathing slowed somewhat as she paused before the doorway to the upstairs. She could not force herself to remain there in the lower hall, or to continue thinking about the image of the bossy witch. A strong warning feeling, almost a presence, emanated from the gathered coven, propelling Henrietta through the now-open door and up the steps. The entrance closed automatically behind her, and Henrietta stumbled her way upward in the dark. No heartening glow preceded her as it had since....

Henrietta realized she had not felt the presence of her talisman since she entered her home. In fact, it seemed to have disappeared. She kept one hand on the stair rail to the right and the other on the wall at the left. In her bedroom, she rapidly closed the door, and fumbled for the light.

Only then did she look down and observe a slight bulge beneath her shirt. Yet, she could not bring herself to touch the amulet beneath her fabric top. Instead, she leaned back against her bedroom door and breathed a deep sigh of relief. She was safe—for now.

What did the presence of her mother's coven with a total of thirteen witches, mean? Was it an evil omen?

Before Henrietta could give that question more serious thought, she noticed a secondary light shining from across her room. As she focused more clearly, she observed the closet doorknob glowing. Unfortunately, she saw something else.

Henrietta's reflection in the mirror revealed a swirling dark mass of intertwined hexes flowing over the surface of her entire body, and yet, she could not reach for her amulet to try and undo the spells placed upon her.

The light-emitting knob drew her attention like a magnet, and Henrietta walked in a daze to her closet door. The glowing handle turned under her grasp and when the door opened on its own she stepped within—not knowing why she'd entered there. The door closed behind her, but the closet was not totally dark inside.

An eerie radiance shone from the back wall behind her hanging clothes. Henrietta wanted to grasp her amulet, but some power restrained her hand. The glimmering at the rear of her enclosure increased, however, and she strengthened her resolve to fight the energy that forbade touching the talisman.

Inch by inch, her right hand moved upward, and when finally it connected with the bulge in her shirt near her tummy, she felt the amulet begin to hum. Her hand clutched it through the fabric and light burned hotly within her body. Then it surged outward and scorched the black swirling masses clinging to her. There was a sizzling sound and a gagging noise, as though the typical shrieks that accompanied spell-reversals had been smothered by the light.

She was free of hexes again. What should she do? Ought she to flee her home and hide in the metal tool shed out back?

The light of her amulet increased even more and shined between the spaces in the clothes hanging on the closet rod, illuminating the rear wall in a bright rectangle running from floor to ceiling. A hidden doorway opened.

A strong positive feeling told her to go through it. Should she?

14: SECRET PASSAGE

Henrietta's hand remained on her amulet. The talisman's light shined brighter than ever, and the clothes before her parted as though unseen hands separated them. The passageway behind the hidden doorway was lighted, just as her room had once lit up.

A lingering urge to return to her bedroom and obey the coven leader's command pulled on Henrietta, but she fought it, whispering, "I am not like them. I am not a witch, and I will not obey."

Still gripping her talisman, she stepped forward past the divided wardrobe, through the previously concealed entryway, to enter an unknown passage. Henrietta could not see very far ahead, and noted the light was brighter to the rear. Turning, she saw a much narrower access-way going in the opposite direction.

She felt she should go there, and as she moved that way, the light disappeared behind her and led Henrietta forth into the narrower passageway. She had to turn sideways to squeeze through, and after a few paces she discovered a tiny set of steps leading downward. The stairs ended in a wider hall, and she followed the light without hesitation.

Two turns later, she was totally disoriented, but the secret passage led straight until she could see it no more. Partway down the hall the illumination dimmed.

In its place, her amulet emitted an intense beam like a strong flashlight, which shined through her shirt and between her splayed fingers. The light was strong enough to turn the edges of her fingers pink where it penetrated her skin. By manipulating her hand, she could control the bright stream to an amazing degree. As she stepped forward, she focused the beam ahead, guiding her.

Why had the hall radiance diminished, and how could she have lived in this house for eleven years and not discovered there were hidden passages? Did her mother know of them?

Henrietta heard faint babbling somewhere ahead and slowed, being sure not to make noise. But before she could actually distinguish spoken words, she found the light from her amulet focused on a small doorway to her right.

Where could that go? Outside perhaps? She had no idea, but obviously the amulet light was signaling her to enter.

Carefully lifting the old fashioned latch, she opened the door. The cramped room lit up and she saw that it contained an old school desk with a sloped top. An ancient book with a leather cover rested on the angled desktop and a smaller book lay atop it. The desk's wooden surface had been scratched and inked with names and initials. The curved seat could be folded up but was currently in the down position.

Henrietta read the ornate lettering on the title of the small, topmost book.

MY DIARY

The fat volume beneath had its title mostly covered so she could not make it out, but the letters she could see were even fancier than those on the top book. No sooner had she noted parts of the title than the light dimmed in the small room.

The glow of her amulet resumed again, but this time it illumined the doorway as a signal for her to leave. Withdrawing from there, the radiance again shined down the straight passage in the way she'd previously been headed. So involved had she been in studying the books, she had ceased to notice the drone of nearby voices.

As Henrietta again proceeded quietly, however, she heard words indistinctly through the wall.

"Then where is she?" That voice sounded like the head of the coven. "She's not in her room."

Henrietta's mother replied, "She's probably out in the metal shed, hiding with her dog."

"Does she know about the book?"

"Of course not, I'm not stupid."

During the silence that followed, Henrietta held her breath. She was so glad Elgin had not come in the house with her. He would have followed down the passageway and might have barked at the sound of voices through the wall.

It was then that Henrietta noticed two pinpoints of light a few feet farther down the hall. With the talisman no longer glowing, and her eyes mostly accustomed to the dark, she saw the mini-beacons clearly.

Shuffling in silence along the wall, she discovered two eye-holes in its surface. They were about one inch in diameter, and spaced just right for viewing the interior of the living room beyond, although she had to stand on tiptoe to do that.

"Are you winning her over to our side...to her destiny?"

"Of course!" That was Henrietta's mother answering too loudly, meaning she did not really believe what she said.

"You know the alternative, Delvettica, if you're wrong. *Sacrifice*...the time of year is almost upon us. She's either one of us, or—"

Delvettica almost screeched, "It doesn't have to be this year; she's only eleven."

"But you know she must be innocent...a virgin."

Henrietta held her breath, feeling shocked and scared. Under other circumstances, she would also be blushing. Anyway, she barely had friends, and only knew one boy, Cory. The coven leader's statement was totally disgusting. But—sacrifice? What had the witch meant by that? Unfortunately for Henrietta, she thought she knew the answer to her own question.

"I'm warning you, Delvettica, if your little witch turns to the other side it will go badly for you *both*. Guard *The Book* with your life. No, never mind. I don't feel comfortable with it remaining here any longer. Fetch it, now!"

15: THE BOOK

If Henrietta had lived with fear for years—and she had—she now experienced a new level of total, muscle-cramping dread. She could not move; she couldn't even breath. Yet, she knew she must not remain there in the dark hallway, stiff as a store mannequin, to be discovered by the coven.

Her mind raced even though her body was paralyzed. What was so important about the book? And which book did the coven leader mean? The big one or the little one?

Henrietta's fingers still touched the wall to balance her on tiptoe. Through the eye-holes, she saw mostly the witches' heads, but even then just the medium-height and taller ones. Another witch rushed into the living room. "She's gone. She's not in the house, and she's not in the shed."

That information caused immediate havoc among the agitated coven.

"Find her—now!"

Even if Henrietta had not seen the lead witch speaking, there was no doubt who had shouted that command.

"She's probably off visiting one of her little friends."

"She has friends?" The venom in those words penetrated the walls of the house.

Delvettica's attempt to soothe her evil leader had backfired, awfully. "Well...not really, I meant—"

"Never mind the book for now. Find the girl and bring her to me. We'll soon get to the bottom of this."

In an instant, the room half-cleared, as witches scattered out the doors on either side.

At the same moment, Henrietta felt the vibration of her talisman against her tummy. Soothing pulsations softened her frozen muscles, and her feet lowered flat on the floor. Henrietta withdrew her hands from the wall and felt her way back in the direction she had come. Her talisman highlighted the door into the miniature room, signaling her to enter.

When she did, she knew what was needed and lifted both books from the desk. She did not hesitate, and although the larger one was quite heavy, she fled the mini-chamber, retracing the lighted path back to her bedroom closet. She was breathing heavily by the time she paused behind her hanging wardrobe.

The sound of witches in her bedroom should have made Henrietta turn and flee, but she was rooted to the spot. The coven leader's voice sneered at her attendants, "So this is the little dear's room? Look! All the spells have been removed. It's as clean as an innocent baby's newly scrubbed face. How did that happen?"

The others all sputtered at once, unable to come up with an answer until one said, "White Magic, perhaps?"

"And she has friends," the bossy witch continued. "What was Delvettica thinking? Her task was simple. Wasn't it simple?"

"Oh yes," one of the other witches replied. "Very simple, your supreme evilness."

"Stop trying to flatter me. We must get to the bottom of this. Everyone to the spell room, now."

Henrietta heard them scrambling for the door, but just as she could finally sigh with relief, the closet entrance was flung wide open and the witch leader glared inside. Studying the clothing hanging on the rod, the woman muttered to herself. Somehow, she did not see Henrietta standing in the darkness just beyond.

"Well, she got the wardrobe right. No self-respecting kid would wear these. The children should have reviled her at school and she should have hated them right back. With her hatred, we will control her. But it does not matter. I'll use the pentagram to summon spirits to do my bidding...they'll find the little witch, and we'll wrap her in spells so dark she'll..."

The coven leader's laughter made Henrietta's arms turn all goose bumpy. But something else happened. The witch's face got a surprised look and she twisted her neck, checking out the room behind her.

As she did so, Henrietta saw through her false surface mask, past the pretty face to the awful image hidden deeper within. Revealed there were the most grotesque features Henrietta had ever seen, but under that was something truly unexpected.

Hidden beneath all the rest was a face so sweet and endearing that any observer would have been won over by it. Preposterous as it seemed, this was the woman's actual face. Somehow, that fact was scarier to Henrietta than all else she had recently seen and heard. This strikingly beautiful witch could use whichever appearance she wished in order to make the desired impression.

After the door slammed loudly, and the witch had left, Henrietta was still covered with goose flesh, her heart pounded in her chest, and her breath came in great gasps.

16: HIDDEN BASEMENT

When Henrietta's fears lessened and her breathing approached normal, thanks to the amulet's pulsing again, she stepped out into her bedroom to find it had been ransacked. Her checkerboard quilt lay in a heap on the floor, with her mattresses upside down on top of it. Keepsakes had been swept from the shelves and scattered across the rug. Her dresser drawers lay askew atop piles of clothing and dolls. Overriding all of the messiness was a black, shadowy mass swarming with the witches' evil spells. The sight made Henrietta nearly vomit.

She had not heard the witches doing all this. How could that be? A thought came to her that *they* had not done all this. She knew intuitively it had mostly been the handiwork of the coven leader when she left the room. If the vile woman had done this to the bedroom in the twinkling of an eye, what could she do to Henrietta over time?

Henrietta plopped down on a section of the wooden floor not covered by the oval rug, but where no hexes were visible. The two books slipped from her weary fingers and clunked to the hard surface. The diary slid off the larger volume revealing a title and author in intricate silver lettering on the big book. She read silently the words:

The Compleat Collectanea of Witchcraft & Demonology by Miss Hester Crawley-Raevan.

The book's age-cracked, leather cover also contained silver-colored symbols associated with conjuring. A small pentagram was visible, along with a tiny figure of the devil that gave Henrietta the chills because of the way its tail snaked around its head.

She had no intention of opening the large book, in fact, she didn't want to touch it again now that she'd seen its cover. Henrietta's hand went automatically to her midriff, grasping the clothespin talisman through the fabric of her top.

The amulet churned with energy and a stream of light poured forth, cradling the larger book with such brilliance she closed her eyes. When the pulsations of her talisman ceased, she looked to see a silvery shimmer engulfing the dark volume.

The wavering light distorted the writing and the figures on the surface of the cover as if it were a desert mirage. The shimmering did not end with the witchcraft volume, however, and extended outward in a line, under the heap of bedding and mattresses, which now tilted up slightly at one side. The light-line continued underneath the pile and she knew what this meant. Henrietta forcefully slid the book along that glowing line and under the mass of bedding, which collapsed back over it, concealing the witchery book.

She wanted to use her amulet to undo all the spells in her room, but it did not respond to her mental urging. Instead, the back of her closet again radiated light, apparently beckoning for her to return there. Henrietta feared one of the witches would come and discover her and since she had no better plan for her safety, she quietly stood up. Retrieving the diary, she entered the hidden passage. Why hadn't she been directed to hide the small book as well? Was she supposed to read it?

Descending to the first floor level, Henrietta was then guided to a second downward stairway, which she found circled back on itself. This ancient set of steps was constructed of bricks, some of which were crumbly, and she took pains not to fall or make noise during her descent.

The lower she traveled down the steep decline, the more she encountered moist, yukky-smelling air, and she worried where the light from the talisman was leading her. At last she reached an ancient brick floor. Surely this predated the house by decades, or even longer.

After minutes of careful walking through a maze of tunnels, she entered a room just as her amulet's light extinguished. Fortunately, there was a dim light from the room above. When Henrietta looked up, she saw what appeared to be a glass ceiling with a large pentagram and other sorcery symbols painted on top of its surface. More accurately, the black arts designs had been applied to the clear floor of the room above.

She first thought that she must be underneath her mother's spell room, but it had no transparent floor, and was in fact on the street level of the house, certainly not this far underground. Obviously, there were subbasements beneath her residence, which—like the hidden tunnels—she had known nothing about.

Henrietta's amulet again whined with expanding energy and its light burst forth, creating a beam that focused on the underside of the transparent ceiling above her. It created a mirror-image pentagram directly beneath the first, in a process that sounded like the noise of a blow torch. This second image glowed brightly at first, and then dimmed to a gentler luminosity. The talisman at last went dormant.

And then it happened–

Witches streamed out onto the overhead floor, causing Henrietta's mouth to fall open. She quickly clenched her teeth and lowered her eyes, since she'd discovered she could see the underclothes of most of the witches—the ones who wore dresses that is—which was way over half of them.

17: THE GREAT HEX

Henrietta remained where she was even though her first impulse was to return through the tunnels, find her way back upstairs, and sneak out of the house. Maybe to hide in the metal shed with Elgin. What had become of her dog, anyway? She hated to think about that. Those horrid witches better not have hurt her little Scottish terrier.

Moving shadows cast from above caused Henrietta to glance upward again where she saw the coven arranging itself on the sorcery pentagram. Their leader stood exactly in the middle with Delvettica, while five witches placed themselves at the tips of the immense, five-pointed star. Meanwhile, the six remaining witches positioned themselves evenly around the circle that formed the outer edge of the pentagram—making a total of thirteen.

The coven leader turned around in place a few times, chanting words Henrietta heard but did not understand. The witch then called out the names of certain spirits, commanding them to come forth and do her bidding. The demons were to locate Delvettica's wayward daughter and hold her captive until the coven could secure her for their satanic rituals. The word "sacrifice" was repeated several times, sending shivers down Henrietta's back.

Clearly, from what Henrietta had previously overheard, it was a summoning of evil spirits. Her state of alarm made it hard to breath, and she wanted to flee. She feared that the head witch, who was now bent over and drawing hex symbols on the floor around her feet, would see Henrietta through the glass. That could happen even in the shadowy subbasement, especially if Henrietta moved. Instinctively, she grasped her talisman through her shirt, but it did not respond. There was no vibration or glowing. Henrietta felt all alone.

High above her, the ceiling of the spell room over the coven seemed to melt as black mists gathered there and swirled lower. Only a few feet above the witches' heads, the dark cloud recoiled as though it had bumped into something solid, although nothing visible was encountered.

The black haze moved downward again, only to retreat once more. The coven leader glared up at the murky haze and screamed more incantations, but the churning shadow world was held at bay by something invisible. Exasperated, the witch turned on Delvettica.

"What have you done? The book is gone from its hiding place...your daughter is missing..." She paused before screeching, "And the pentagram doesn't work!"

Shoving Delvettica out of the protective circle, the lead witch pointed her arm straight, aiming her index finger at Henrietta's mother, "By all that is *unholy*, I curse you through time immemorial."

Henrietta gasped when her mother fell to the floor unconscious.

The hexing continued in a higher-pitched voice, "Your body will be covered with oozing boils, your hair will fall out...you will become a deaf and dumb mute.... Your eyes will stare sightless at a blank world. All who see you will shrink away in abhorrence...especially your daughter."

Henrietta thought of what had happened to the teacher, Mr. Baxter, and shivered even more.

All the witches stared expectantly at the motionless form on the floor.

Henrietta guessed they wanted to see her mother covered immediately in hideous boils. Whatever their expectation, it was taking longer than the witches had anticipated.

The coven leader jumped up and down. "This can't be happening. Curse this house and all who reside here...from now until *forever*."

The other witches continued staring at the still form of Henrietta's mother. One of them said in amazement, "It's not working. The spell is not controlling her."

The witches backed silently away from Delvettica, abandoning the pentagram and glancing around apprehensively, then filed one at a time from the room. The dark swirls above their heads had disappeared, though the witches seemed not to notice.

18: THE DIARY

Henrietta continued staring upward at her mother's body lying prostate on the glass floor. Delvettica had not moved, and the side of her face pressed against the clear surface, flattening her cheek like a large plastic suction cup stuck to a refrigerator. Drool seeped from her open mouth, puddling onto the glass, and looking really gross.

Was Henrietta's mother still alive? On closer inspection, Delvettica's abdomen gently moved in and out. Although there were no visible signs of boils, the deaf and dumb portions of the awful hexing might be manifesting. Henrietta shuddered and looked away.

Only then did she feel the weight of the book in her hand. Because of the dim light, she raised the small volume up close to her eyes and made out the gold-leafed title, *My Diary*.

Pulling open the cover, she saw on the first page a printed line that read *This Diary Belongs to:*

And following on the space immediately below those words was a long underline–originally blank. Above which was neatly handwritten in oversized cursive *Delvettica H. House*. Henrietta had the same middle name as her mother. Below that was inked in parentheses *(Age Thirteen).* The blue ink was difficult to make out in the poor light and Henrietta had to squint and study it for a moment to read the last part. This was definitely her mother's diary.

Curious as Henrietta was to know what her mother had written in it, she needed to find out whether the coven was still in the house, and if Elgin was safe.

Henrietta returned to the dark passageways and they lighted automatically ahead of her, darkening once more behind. When she arrived at the rear of her clothes closet, she breathed heavily and sweat trickled down the side of her forehead. Something told her the coven had evacuated her home, hopefully, never to return.

Elgin lay unmoving on the rug in her room. His position reminded Henrietta of how her mother lay on the secret room's clear sorcery surface. He breathed with difficulty and a black fog engulfed his body.

Henrietta grasped her amulet and it churned to life, immediately building up a great charge of energy that surged out to surround the darkness on her dog. The murkiness fought back, but in the end it weakened and dissolved, leaving her pet breathing much easier.

In the next few minutes, Henrietta used her talisman to remove all the spells evident in her bedroom, and then she tugged her mattress and box springs back onto their frame. Retrieving the large volume from beneath the bedding on the floor, she slid it under her bed out of sight. Sensing that her mother and Elgin needed to sleep off the effects of witchcraft, she carefully lifted her Scottish terrier onto the pile of blankets and sheets she had replaced on her bed. He did not waken, but curled into a ball and began to snore softly.

Henrietta propped herself against the headboard with pillows, and settled back to study the slender diary. Opening the next page after her mother's signature, she read:

Dear Diary,

I have no one to talk to. I don't know why mother hates me. Why does she make everyone else hate me too? I never wanted to be a witch. I don't want to be like her, but the ugly hag treats me awful! Now I hate her back. I want to get even.

If I ever get my hands on her big book of spells, I'll show her what it's like. I think she's coming. I've got to find a good hiding place for you.

I'll write more later—

Henrietta tilted her head back and stared up at the ceiling. From what she'd just read, her mother's childhood had been just as messed-up as Henrietta's. Still, that was no excuse for a mother to treat her own daughter the same way. Henrietta turned the page—

Dear Diary,

Sorry I didn't write sooner. Mom's been snooping around like she knew I had a diary and she wanted to find it.

I discovered this little room in the hidden lower passages. Mom doesn't know about it. Even if she did know, this area is covered in cobwebs and she hates spiders so she'll never visit this place. I'll keep you here and sneak down to write some more whenever I can.

The next entry read:

Dear Diary, today at school I fixed Kaleen good. She's been mean to me for months, but no more. I went in the restroom at lunchtime and used all my hatred to make a spell. I cursed her with zits and boils. By the time lunch was over she had an outbreak of pimples all over her face and was getting a boil on her arm. The nurse said it was the worst case of skin eruptions she'd ever seen and couldn't figure out how it happened so fast. Ha Ha!

When I looked in the bathroom mirror before I went out to the playground I saw a wart starting to grow near the end of my nose. It's not too big. I think maybe it came because of all the black magic I've been doing to get even with the other kids. I don't care. It's worth it!

Henrietta closed her mother's diary. She had goose bumps on her arms. Her grandmother had done to Delvettica what Delvettica was now doing to Henrietta. That was totally messed up. Henrietta would never do that to a daughter–if she ever had one.

She set the diary down and made herself relax the over-tense muscles throughout her body. She sighed deeply and thought about all that had recently happened.

Luckily for Henrietta, the amulet seemed to be more powerful than the entire coven put together. If it had not been for the lighted pentagram the amulet made underneath the dark one painted on the glass floor, she'd have been discovered by the witches and might already have been sacrificed.

With that thought, tension returned to her body. She needed a place to hide her mother's diary and the big book the coven was after. But where?

19: MEETING HAZEL

Henrietta's initial thought was to hide the books out in the storage shed, but she knew that was the first place her mother would look, assuming she returned to normal. If her mother was still "sleeping" in another day, Henrietta would have to call an ambulance for help.

How would she get her mother out of that awful lower room? She couldn't let ambulance attendants go down there. Hopefully, her mom would get better on her own. Elgin was a different matter. She could carry him to the veterinarian if she needed to.

Henrietta finally hid the two books in the downstairs bathroom. There was a big linen closet in there, stuffed full of fabric items. She slipped the volumes underneath sheets, pillow cases, crocheted doilies, and miscellaneous things that looked to be at least one hundred years old. Then she used the talisman to blast the entire room with white light. When she was done, a silvery shimmer covered everything.

Henrietta went back down the passageways again and gazed up through the glass floor at her mother.

Delvettica had rolled over on her side. She seemed to be sleeping peacefully, and when Henrietta touched her talisman, nothing happened.

Returning to her bedroom, she found Elgin was sleeping on his back with all four legs pointing up in the air. She chuckled.

The following day, Henrietta took some money from the kitchen drawer where Delvettica kept the small grocery fund for when she made her daughter walk to the store to get whatever struck her fancy.

Henrietta wasn't going to pack a lunch today. She would purchase hot lunch instead–for the first time *ever*. Her mother always made her pack a lunch that was guaranteed to turn the other kids' stomachs, and promote maximum ridicule.

"Ooh," they'd say, "You're going to eat that? It's nasty!"

They were right. It was always revolting.

There was a bounce in her step as Henrietta walked to school that morning with her backpack slung over one shoulder. She couldn't wait to get to her classroom because nothing that could happen there would be nearly as bad as what she'd been experiencing at home. Also, things could be better back home by the time she finished her school day.

She had only gone about a block when she decided to turn south to the city park. A similar impulse had caused her to put her mother's diary in her book bag just before she left the house. Henrietta was going to get to school early anyway, so she had time to do a small stint on the swings. There might be kids on the swing set over at the school, even this early, and right now she wanted to be alone.

Henrietta was right, the park was totally empty, no people anywhere, but she did notice a black and white pigeon pecking around for food only twenty feet from the swing set where she was headed.

She wondered what it could be eating. Maybe someone had dropped some popcorn on the ground? Most wild pigeons that came to the park were gray. Maybe this one was somebody's pet. The nearer she got, the odder it seemed that the bird didn't fly away.

Henrietta dropped her pack and settled into a swing. The pigeon was barely six feet away, bustling around to gather whatever it was eating.

A woman's voice said unexpectedly, "That pigeon belongs to someone."

After the events of the previous day, Henrietta nearly jumped right out of her skin. She turned to see a middle-aged woman, slightly overweight, but with a smile that put Henrietta immediately at ease.

"That's what I thought too," said Henrietta.

The woman clucked her tongue twice. "You know, dear, I said that because I recognize this pigeon. It belongs to my young friend."

"Really?"

"Yes."

The bird leaped into the air just then. Flapping over some shrubbery, it flew toward the large, brick, bank building, and disappeared from sight.

Henrietta turned back to the lady who had seated herself in one of the swing seats.

"That's a very unusual pigeon," said the woman. "Oh, by the way, my name is Hazel."

Henrietta's mother had never warned her to stay away from strangers. In fact, Delvettica might have encouraged that if she'd thought it could happen. Potentially, such circumstances might create more of a witch-like mindset in Henrietta through a calamity.

"You look like you've had a rough time lately," added Hazel.

Henrietta wondered for a moment where the woman had come from, since the park was obviously empty when she'd entered it, except for the pigeon. But before she knew it, Henrietta found herself confiding in this person she'd never seen before.

"My mother is hard to get along with sometimes, almost always, actually...and her friends are worse."

Hazel clucked her tongue again. "That's too bad, but maybe you will discover something that will help you to understand her."

"I already have," Henrietta replied.

"Oh?"

"I've found my mom's diary...from when she was thirteen."

"That's a troublesome age for anyone."

"I suppose. I'm only eleven."

"A lot can happen in eleven years."

Henrietta found herself reviewing her life in fast-forward, from her earliest memories right up to the present. Things seemed to be getting worse, not better, except for the talisman. Thank goodness for that. She absently removed one hand from the swing's chain, and felt for her amulet under her shirt.

Her reverie was broken when Hazel said, "Life is not always B & W...that means black and white."

For some reason, when Henrietta heard that statement she thought first of her bedspread and then about the black and white pigeon.

After that, she thought of the coven of witches positioned around the pentagram, trying to summon evil spirits to find Henrietta and do things to her that she did not want to even think about.

She shuddered involuntarily, and the hand still holding her talisman squeezed it. The amulet vibrated and energy grew within Henrietta.

"It's not you who needs to be afraid," said Hazel, staring at the hand grasping the hidden talisman as though she could see the light it emitted. "An amulet, you know, is nothing but a focus for one's *own* power. Without the person, the amulet is nothing."

For some reason, those words jarred Henrietta deep inside.

"When the right person picks up their talisman, something magical happens. The truth is, no one can hurt you now...but yourself."

"What?" Henrietta did not understand that.

"You are at a fork in the road. One path leads to darkness, the other leads to light, and although it seems that anyone could easily distinguish from those two, the reality is not really so clear.

"If you fight evil, it becomes stronger and you are pulled down that path along with it."

Henrietta blinked at the woman because she did not understand her meaning.

"Oh, it will come to you after I leave.

"Henrietta, I would like for us to be friends—if you want that too—and I will visit again if its okay."

Henrietta nodded. "I don't really have any friends, I don't think."

"You do now."

The truth Henrietta felt in those words brought tears to her eyes. She stopped her swing and wiped them away with her hands. When her eyelids opened a moment later, Hazel had left.

Henrietta scanned the perimeter of the park, but the woman was nowhere about. It seemed impossible she could have departed so quickly.

20: B & W FRIENDSHIP

It did not surprise Henrietta when her supposedly "new" friends Tabitha, Cory and Adelle pretended not to know her as she entered the school. It also did not shock her when Cory and Adelle continued to look around at everyone but Henrietta once they were in the classroom. And it likewise wasn't out of place for Allie and Janna to once again treat her like she was their long lost friend. At least for the start of the day.

Henrietta put her backpack on top of her desk and plopped into her seat.

"Where were you after school?" Allie asked while leaning over Henrietta's desk, with her hands resting on the wood surface.

"I had to go home," Henrietta said casually, just the way she thought Allie would have responded if their positions were reversed. She looked her "old friend" directly in the eye. What ran through her mind was the vision of Allie and Janna driving away yesterday after school.

Allie smiled brightly, and said, "Oh. See you later," then turned and left in a hurry.

The rest of the morning went without a hitch until first recess. On the playground, no one was mean to Henrietta, but it was, once again, as if she did not exist. That had to be the work of Allie and Janna. It hurt more now because she'd experienced what she thought was friendship and had cherished it for a couple of days.

Cory was doing his finest nerd impersonations, and Adelle hung out on the periphery of Tabitha's group, without actually being part of it. Tabitha was, as usual, queen bee of the playground, with a cluster of kids from several classes gathered about her.

Allie and Janna were off to one side, apparently studying together, although Henrietta thought it more likely they were plotting.

She went over to swing, and when next she looked at the dragon twins—as she now termed them thanks to Cory—her suspicions were confirmed. A growing trickle of other kids made their way in ones, twos or small groups to go into a huddle with Allie and Janna.

They giggled together about something they were looking at, and occasionally one would glance furtively in Henrietta's direction, but when they saw her looking back, they turned hastily away.

What now? Part of Henrietta wanted to jog over there and see what they were up to. Another part didn't wish to lower herself.

A few minutes went by and Adelle showed up at the swing set, clearly avoiding Henrietta with her eyes and the positioning of her body, but whispering to get her attention. "Meet me in the restroom, and hurry."

Adelle strolled off, headed away from the school, but Henrietta noticed she soon veered around toward the building.

Does she think I'm that stupid? Nobody is going to make a fool out of me again.

Just as Henrietta thought of that, her amulet began to hum. Should I go and meet Adelle? she wondered. The amulet vibrated even more, and Henrietta headed for the school as if she might be thirsty.

A quick glance at the group huddled around Allie and Janna told her no one had noticed her leaving the playground.

Inside the building, the amulet sent a glowing path in front of her to the girl's restroom. With that prompt, she nearly *ran* inside. Adelle pretended not to notice her until two other girls left. Then she burst out, "They've got your mom's diary."

Henrietta felt like she'd been plunged into frigid water. She didn't think anything but the coven's curses could hit her as hard as this news had.

She recalled Allie leaning over her desk above her backpack. How could she do that? The little thief! Henrietta felt completely violated. It was like this girl had a sixth sense for finding anyone's weakness. Henrietta was furious. She glanced in the mirror and saw her face was beet red.

"I'll..." she began, and the images running through her mind were at once black and dire as she thought of how she would make the girls pay.

Her mother's zits and boils curse flashed into mind. That would be fine for a start. Allie and Janna would be spending so much time at the dermatologist's they'd have none left for plotting.

"Cory's on it," said Adelle. "Stay in here, because what the Dragon Twins want is for you to do something really stupid, and get yourself in deep trouble."

"But they stole..."

"Cory will get it back, don't worry."

Henrietta was not in a mood to be pacified. "What's he going to do, pull the fire alarm again?"

"Nope," Adelle laughed. "That's *our* job."

21: FALSE ALARM

As Adelle checked her watch for seemingly the fiftieth time, Henrietta paced the lavatory floor. "I shouldn't just sit in here, and we can't pull the..."

"It's time now," Adelle grabbed Henrietta's arm and jerked her through the doorway. "You want to ring it?"

Despite Henrietta's previous misgivings, she yanked the alarm lever with so much force she thought she'd dislocated her shoulder.

Adelle dragged her back into the girl's bathroom. "Quick, hide in a stall. If they catch us, we'll burn for the other false alarm too."

Henrietta tried to control her breathing after she locked the stall door and climbed up on top of the toilet so no one would be able to see her by glancing quickly under the partition walls.

All at once, she wished she'd never left home in the morning—except for meeting Hazel, that is. When she thought of that woman, she relaxed. This time she surely did have a friend. When she imagined friendship, Adelle came into her mind, along with Cory and Tabitha. Maybe they really were her friends. She felt her talisman humming again.

The door to the next stall creaked and Adelle said, "Hurry, if we take too long getting out there, they'll know it was us."

Henrietta could not keep up with her accomplice until they reached the outside doorway where Adelle slowed and walked calmly outside. Henrietta lengthened her pace to catch up. When they neared the lines of students standing in neat rows at the far end of the playground, an instructional assistant strode out to meet them.

"Where were you two?"

Adelle shrugged. "The bathroom. You know I..."

"And what about you?"

Henrietta, stammered, "I was–"

"Helping me..." said Adelle, while grabbing her middle and leaning over.

"Well," said the woman, "hurry and get in line."

As they made their way between two rows of students, Henrietta glimpsed Allie trampling about just one line over—looking at the ground as though she had lost something. Henrietta found a gap in the line to join her class, and someone bumped into her, pressing a flat object against her middle.

Her Amulet churned with energy and she feared something or someone was attempting to take the talisman from her, but then she realized the object thrust upon her was her mother's diary.

She looked up as she slipped it underneath her shirt, just in time to see Cory ducking between two kids a half-dozen paces beyond her.

This guy was anything but a nerd. Same with Adelle, she'd played her "handicap" like it was a winning card.

When they were all back in class, there was bickering between Allie and Janna. Henrietta could only guess what that was about, but it likely had to do with the diary she again possessed. Her *real* friends pretended not to notice her, and for the first time, that was more than all right.

Henrietta got a restroom pass and when she was safe in a lavatory stall she sat down to leaf through the pages of her mother's diary. Allie better not have damaged it! Henrietta felt like that was such a terrible violation, others having read it. The little book seemed to be okay. She turned to the third entry page and read:

Dear Diary,

*I have hated my mother. I hate her coven. And I will hate Kaleen to her dying day, which is likely to be sooner than she ever expected. But there's more to it than that. I detest myself and what I have become. They have made me into one of them. I hate them for it but I can't stop. It feels too good to get even with all the people I loathe! And now that I've found **The Book** I can't wait to see what I will do with its knowledge. My wart grows more each day and my* *nose is becoming hideous, but with the new sorcery I will avenge myself on all who tease and despise me. I no longer look in the mirror if I can help it.*

Although Henrietta had intended to read more, that was all she could stand for the moment.

She returned to the classroom with the diary stuck safely underneath her clothes. For once, she was thankful for the baggy pants her mother had picked out for her to wear.

For the first time since she could remember, Henrietta hated her mother a bit less. She also hated Allie and Janna somewhat less as well. Maybe she could not forgive them, but perhaps she could keep from getting even with them the way her mother had done to Kaleen.

22: TURNABOUT

To Henrietta's great surprise, Allie and Janna were waiting for her after school so she could walk home with them. She was so flabbergasted that she did not tell them no, instead, she answered, "I can only walk partway, because my mom's not feeling well again."

"That's too bad," said Allie, sounding genuinely compassionate.

What were these girls made of? It sure wasn't like in the old rhyme "...sugar and spice and everything nice."

In the same day, these two had made fun of Henrietta and her mother, and now they were sympathetic? There was no figuring them out.

"I guess the joke's on us," said Janna.

Henrietta was puzzled. "How's that?"

"Well, the fake *Diary of a Witch* you made for your special project was so good that it fooled everyone, including us."

Henrietta's mind raced like a demon fleeing holy water, "Oh, yeah...that. How'd you guys figure it out?"

"Tabitha told us," said Janna.

Allie added, "For a little while, we were the laughing stocks of the school."

"Yeah," Janna said, "some kids started whispering that *we* were nerds."

Allie gulped loudly and then said, "You fooled us at first. But we weren't trying to hurt you. Not really. Just having some fun."

Henrietta said, "It looks like it turned out not to be so much fun—for you.

"Here's where I head home. See you tomorrow."

She smiled to herself as she crossed the street.

"See you," the other two called in unison.

When they were out of sight, Henrietta turned toward the park. She wasn't ready to go home yet, because she worried what she'd find there. She needed to do some thinking before she checked on her mother.

What if her mom was back to normal? Henrietta had a lot of freedom when her mother was unconscious. Today, she'd had hot lunch at school for the first time.

In the city park, Henrietta slipped her mother's diary out from under her clothing and returned it to her backpack. She saw that same white and black pigeon fly down beside the swing set as she neared.

She was not surprised when the bird didn't fly away even though she got within three feet of where it searched for food.

There were a few people at the park during this visit–mostly little kids.

While seating herself in a swing, it seemed only natural to hear Hazel's voice beside her. "Sometimes the park is a nice place to come and get away from the rest of your life."

Henrietta looked over to see Hazel's smiling face, but she noted there was also concern there as well. "Hi," Henrietta said, as she lowered her backpack to the ground and began to swing.

"Children these days," Hazel said, "too often carry burdens that are way beyond their years." She looked down at Henrietta's bag resting on the ground and then lifted up her feet, leaned back, and began to swing as well. "It often relaxes me to come here and sail back and forth through the air like this." She sighed.

Henrietta took a deep breath, as well.

After a few minutes of swinging, Hazel said, "My dear girl, you need to know that the Almighty created the *real* magic, and our religions call it miracles. The medical profession terms it spontaneous remission. Witches say it is black or white magic...and other sciences...

"Oh, my. Just listen to me carrying on. You need to just keep swinging...and relax. Don't pay too much attention to what some old lady in the park tries to tell you. And for sure, don't worry about kids calling you things like 'that Little Witch Girl.'"

Henrietta had mostly missed out on hearing the *witch girl* reference because when she heard the words "spontaneous remission," her mind got tangled up on that thought. Hope grew within her. Perhaps her mother would be awake and healthy when Henrietta returned home.

After swinging for a bit, she asked Hazel, "Does white magic really exist?"

"Yes. But not the way most people imagine. It comes in a form of love. One of the highest forms. That is the real magic, and in this old world of ours, there is never enough of it to go around."

"Are there covens of white witches?" Henrietta asked. She stopped swinging and looked at Hazel, awaiting her answer.

The woman clucked her tongue. "In what some people term white magic, there are no covens, but there is a kinship between those people, whom others might call white witches. Various names have been used in referring to them."

"Are you a white witch?"

"Interesting question. I can't honestly say 'Yes,' but I can't accurately say 'No,' either. Let's just agree that we are a lot alike, you and I, and neither of us wants to dabble in black magic. Others want to force us into that world if they can. I'm sorry to beat around the bush like this. The truth is, one of us is a white witch...and it is not me."

Henrietta was glad she had stopped swinging—with her feet steady on the ground—otherwise, she might have fallen out of her seat. "I'm a white witch?"

"Yes, dear, I'm afraid so, but it is not an easy road to travel, as you are already finding out. You have more sorcery in your little pinkie than most witches have in their entire bodies. The power is in *you*, not in your amulet. Use it well, but stay away from black magic.

"Your mother's diary is your best teacher about what *not* to do, so keep studying that. But, whatever happens, don't open that awful old book *The Compleat Collectanea of Witchcraft & Demonology*, nor should you let it fall into the wrong hands. You must safeguard it."

Henrietta studied the ground, muttering "I'm a white witch," to herself. She wondered how Hazel knew about *the book* and had so much knowledge of Henrietta's life, but when she turned back to ask, she was gone.

Hazel had disappeared again.

23: AND THEN, BOO

At home, Henrietta found Elgin waiting for her just inside of the front gate. He'd obviously used the pet door to exit the house and seemed none the worse for the now-dissolved spells. He sat there wagging his tail with a pleasant grin on his little Scotty face.

"You missed me, didn't you?" Henrietta asked.

In response, he gave a happy little snarl, followed by a yapping sound.

Before passing through the gateway, however, Henrietta thought of her amulet while focusing on the satanic symbols embedded in the decorative wrought iron design. Now that she'd identified the dubious origin of the symbols, she wanted no part of them.

Energy churned deep within her body, building intensity until it flowed out in a stream of white light, engulfing the metal. The iron grill-work glowed red, then blue, and finally white hot. The symbols twisted and transformed to become nothing more than ornamental flutes and elongated leaf patterns. Still glowing, the front gate opened of its own accord, allowing Henrietta to enter.

Elgin raced ahead to the front door of the house and as Henrietta climbed the steps behind him, she tried to recall if the energy had begun inside her, or if it had originated from her talisman. As best she could determine, the energy began *inside* of her. Hazel must be right, although when Henrietta had first used the amulet, the power seemed to come from it.

"The force is now in me," she whispered in wonder. Then she thought of the diary in her backpack. If she was not careful, she might end up just like her mother.

Turning her front door knob, Henrietta entered the vestibule and heard a creaking sound from the living room. Quietly, she closed the entrance and proceeded inward to the front room where she peeked in to see her mother rocking-away in the old rocking chair that had been stored up in the attic ever since Henrietta could remember. The ancient overstuffed chair her mother usually sat in was nowhere to be seen.

Delvettica looked to be about thirty-five years of age, where before she'd appeared more like fifty-five. There was a childlike innocence on her face and her nose was fairly normal looking, with no sign of a hideous wart.

"Hello dear," said her mother. "Did you have a nice day at school?"

Henrietta nodded her head, and then managed a squeaky, "Uh-huh."

This was not the mother Henrietta had known. In the past, her mom's only inquiries were related to Henrietta's problems with her peers and their many injustices to her.

"We had a visitor," Delvettica said. "Such a nice woman. For some reason, I can't remember her name...or what she looked like. But she helped me take that awful old chair up to the attic and bring down this one. My favorite as a little girl." She sighed with pleasure as she tilted rhythmically, forward-and-back in her rocker.

Because the coven had previously been there, Henrietta looked suspiciously about the living room, but there were no signs of black sorcery, no misty dark spots anywhere. Instead, the front drapes were wide open, allowing sunshine to stream in the leaded windows.

"Run get a snack," said her mother. "You must be starved. Maybe we'll go out for dinner tonight."

Henrietta was stunned. They had *never* gone out to a restaurant—not once in Henrietta's entire life. She walked absently into the hall toward the kitchen, but stopped off in the bathroom, where she checked to be certain that horrid book was still hidden under the linen. It was.

In the kitchen, although Henrietta had hoped otherwise, there was no more food than usual; there were only the same drab choices. Except for a single large red apple sitting in plain sight on the drain board. The kind of apple Snow White had been tricked into eating. That was just a story, Henrietta thought, but she did not take a bite from the apple even though it looked inviting.

Feeling a breeze, Henrietta glimpsed the window and found it was wide open. Her mother always kept the house closed-up tight and it was invariably stuffy, and smelled of powerful herbs, especially in the kitchen. Now, however, the herb aromas were much reduced, and further modified by the scent of hothouse roses. Where had those come from? Henrietta glanced at the ever-empty fruit bowl and discovered it was full of fragrant potpourri.

Who was the mystery visitor her mother had spoken of?

Elgin whined at Henrietta's feet and trotted anxiously around her with his little toenails clicking on the tiles. He yipped in frustration and ran for the back door.

Henrietta thought maybe he had to go potty, and started moving to the rear entrance to let him out, wondering why he didn't simply use the pet door. But what felt like a giant fist clobbered her in the gut. The wind was knocked from her and she fell to the floor unable to breath. She lay there writhing in pain, clutching her stomach, knowing she would soon pass out from lack of oxygen.

Still gripping her tummy, she tried once more to gasp for breath. No air entered her lungs.

Was she about to die? It seemed that nothing could stop that outcome. The course of her life flashed through Henrietta's mind. She briefly relived her early lack of nurturing, living in fear of her mother, painfully giving up her toys, wearing awful clothes, and finally being driven from her bedroom to live in the metal shed. Henrietta had no friends for years, and endured incessant teasing, plus not having a father, and watching Mr. Baxter wither away....

The agony of her life was crushing Henrietta, literally killing her. The brief number of her years had been long in suffering. It was so unfair. When she thought of that, she wondered why she had not done as her mother wanted. Why had she not flung herself to the dark side, repaying all who'd persecuted her?

In a final desperate act, she tried to grasp her talisman. It was gone. There was no amulet or even a string around her neck. Her hope disappeared with it.

Elgin appeared and rushed at her middle, snarling, teeth bared, but was thrown across the room by some unseen force, crashing against the kitchen wall. In Henrietta's final moment, she looked at her small dog, wishing she could help her loyal friend.

The invisible grip squeezed Henrietta even more. Whatever small amount of air she might have had to survive on vanished and her eyes closed. Her mind went blank and darkness swallowed her.

In that last moment, as her life was in final release, Henrietta heard a distant cackling.

24: COVEN'S RETURN

Consciousness was gone. Only a small voice resided in the dark empty place—all that remained of Henrietta's mind.

'*The coven has returned,*' said the tiny voice. '*Remember what Hazel told you. The talisman got its power from you. Use all your might.*'

With that reference to Hazel, a glimmer of hope ignited in Henrietta.

'*You have the power,*' said the whispering voice, "*use it.*"

Henrietta remembered her recent discovery that the energy began from inside her, not from the talisman. She felt a vibration in her middle and a churning sound engulfed her entire body. The power grew rapidly, loosening the death grip around her.

She gasped for air and it entered her lungs. The force grew more potent within her and light filled the kitchen. The dark-conjured spirit, or whatever the vile form was, twisted away from her body and fell to the floor, wriggling, apparently in death's embrace.

In another minute, Henrietta breathed more regularly and was able to sit up. Light-energy bombarded the black mass and it burned in agony, screaming awful oaths, which Henrietta could not understand. Then it disappeared.

Elgin trotted over, tail wagging.

Henrietta heard the small voice again in her mind, *'It's about time.'*

She stared at her pet. No, it couldn't be....

'Why not?' the voice asked.

"Elgin, can you talk?"

He barked in response and ran down the hall toward the living room. *'Hurry,'* the strained voice called in her mind.

Shaking her head, Henrietta got to her feet, took a deep breath and followed him.

'The coven has returned,' said the high-pitched voice. *'Your mother is dying. Get here quick.'*

Henrietta found her mother sprawled out once more in the living room beside the fallen-over rocker. Her mom seemed not to breath, and there was a black shape clinging to her. The same sort that had attacked Henrietta.

Delvettica's body convulsed and a final agonized moan left her lips.

Henrietta's arms raised from her sides, pausing automatically in front of her mid-section. She did not stop to question her subconscious action. Energy grew in her solar plexus and she flung her arms forward at her mother's prostrate form. The expanding force plumed from Henrietta in a bright beam of light, immediately surrounding the dark shape that strangled her mother's spirit.

The murky form fought back, then screamed and shriveled, finally turning into dust. With a last wail, it totally disappeared into nothingness.

Delvettica's breathing resumed, though she remained listless.

Elgin barked again as he left the living room, charging into the entry parlor. *'Hurry!'*

Henrietta ran after him, and as she approached the front entrance where he waited, his rough coat bristling, the door somehow flung open, and he raced out onto the porch, growling ferociously.

Reaching the entry stoop, Henrietta paused. Elgin had raced ahead toward the hedge gate. Its wrought iron once more glowed as if immersed in a bed of blacksmith's coals, which seemed to be tied to the churning in Henrietta's mid-section. Through the gap in the hedge above the gate, Henrietta saw part of the coven standing just across the street. She guessed they were all present, but the shrubbery concealed some members from her view.

The witch leader stood in their midst, glaring at Henrietta. "You are doomed!" she screamed shrilly. "You and your pathetic little dog."

The witch pointed at Henrietta, and something about the way she held her hand out, her finger threatening, brought chills with it. "Give us The Black Book of Spells!"

The menacing arm raised in the air, pointing straight overhead.

Henrietta could not help but follow that motion with her eyes. Looking upward at the sky she saw a dark cloud bank rapidly approaching from the north. Wind whistled and the hedge swayed as the storm surged forward, seemingly aimed at Henrietta's home. Glancing back down at the coven, she saw the witch leader glaring at her, a sneer on her lips.

Gusts of wind slapped Henrietta's face, accompanied by frozen rain that pelted her skin like a shotgun blast—even though it was the wrong time of year for ice.

She tried not to lower her head–knowing she must maintain contact and continue facing the witches, but her eyes watered excessively, and she flinched away in pain. When next she could look toward the coven, the witch leader was crossing the street in her direction. Henrietta stumbled backward, unable to help herself.

'*Use your power,*' Elgin's small voice encouraged.

Henrietta wanted to flee. What could an eleven-year-old do against an entire coven? Perhaps they would go away if she gave them the horrid black book.

'*They will kill us all if you do not act,*' said the tiny voice. '*They plan to sacrifice you. Remember what Hazel said, you have more power in your pinkie....*'

How did he know that? Henrietta stood her ground and looked beyond the gate at the nearing witch. The rest of the coven chanted in the background, but the head witch had paused outside the front yard entrance, which still glowed fiercely just as it had when Henrietta altered its design.

Apparently, even a powerful witch could not pass through it in that glimmering state. Possibly, it was due to the removal of satanic symbols, or maybe the witch's reluctance was from the eerie glow. Henrietta's hope increased, seeing the coven stymied. Elgin stood his ground just inside the gate.

With rekindled hopefulness came a blossoming of the force inside Henrietta. She moved forward to protect her brave little dog. The bright energy spilled out of her in an ever greater wave of power that rose in a tall column, straight up in the air above her home, advancing to meet the conjured storm.

Those light and dark forces collided above the witches, who stood screaming incantations and gesturing threats at Henrietta.

To her great surprise, the coven-generated, stormy darkness included a tornado, yet it could not suppress the light, and began to retreat. The witches were bombarded as the summoned tempest receded. Winds lashed at them just as they had done to Henrietta. The coven shrank back when the wall of frozen rain assailed them. No longer were they threatening her. Disheartened and disheveled, they looked to one another for support, but found none.

Henrietta saw their vanquished state and called up her internal energy even more. She would defeat them and set her mother free—plus, protect her home and save Elgin and herself in the process. This bright counter-offensive flared as it put pressure against the witch's storm front. The pathetic-looking coven did not deserve her sympathy. She would drive them away once and for all.

Henrietta's hair rose from static electricity as her flow of light and energy increased.

Yet, the murkiness that had retreated behind the witches, somehow rallied, shooting spears of lightning in all directions, some of which stabbed into the column of light that Henrietta wielded. Those bolts also struck the roadway near the coven and the witches cowered in fear.

It served them right, Henrietta thought. Now they would get what was coming to them. But the storm strengthened, and began once more advancing toward her home. Winds of hurricane force blasted the coven, stripping loose articles of clothing from the witches, and flinging it away. Frozen rain beat down, reddening their exposed skin. The roof on the house behind them began to separate from the building.

Henrietta gloated. She would show them. The storm, however, continued to move onward, buffeting against the hedge in her yard, and threatening to spill over the top of her house.

Except, a curious thing occurred just then—

Henrietta saw a smile on the coven leader's face. Why would she be smiling? Probably, it was from the prospect of having their storm prevail over Henrietta. Well, she would show them.

The two great forces–light and darkness–rallied on either side. So immense was the struggle that swirling winds completely tore off part of the house roof directly across the street. That section flew out of sight.

The coven was in jeopardy, yet still their leader smiled with satisfaction.

In that moment, Henrietta knew the truth. The coven no longer commanded the gale, she did. *Her* hatred toward the witches now fueled the thunderstorm. The great force of light on her side of the street was diminishing as her negative thoughts caused the storm's resurgence.

And yet, even with that understanding, she could not let go of her dark feelings for the witches, because of what they had tried to do to her and Elgin. This inner fury, if it continued, would destroy not only the coven but much of the town. Henrietta would be responsible for wholesale destruction and the loss of life that accompanied it.

Passing the street and sidewalk, the great tempest moved onward. Fear gripped Henrietta as the storm whipped her hedge, and crossed into her yard, slashing at Elgin's hair.

The witches gloated.

Oh yeah? She would show them!

Even as she attempted to destroy the coven, the storm moved closer yet.

In that second, Henrietta knew she was doing just what they wanted. She was falling into their trap, but she could not stop herself. Hatred of them controlled her.

A burst of wind flung Elgin against the wall of the house. He lay unconscious, and the cyclone's suction pulled at Henrietta, threatening to do the same thing to her. She had powers others only dreamed of, yet she could not control herself. In another moment, she would likely self-destruct.

"You are one of us now!" the coven leader's voice carried above the tempest of the blizzard, for snow had joined with the frozen rain as the temperature dropped below the freezing point. Henrietta looked past the partly-destroyed hedge and saw the gleeful witches. But something in addition caught her eye across the street. A great shaft of light shone downward through the center of the storm.

Hazel stood where that beam touched the ground. She was calm as ever, and seeing her placid face reassured Henrietta. She did not have to fall into the coven's trap, becoming one of their members. She could choose a different path.

Hazel smiled at Henrietta, who smiled back. That moment of respite helped to turn the tide of events away from disaster. The winds died, and the black clouds receded.

The disheveled witches remained in the street looking lost and forlorn. The roadway around them resembled a war zone. Asphalt shingles, boards and chunks of houses littered the pavement and neighboring yards.

Henrietta remembered her dog, ran over and scooped the Scotty into her arms. He was unconscious, but still breathing. Glancing across the road, the sunbeam was gone, and Hazel with it.

The coven of witches marched down the street, trying to avoid debris. They all tramped away except for one member. Their coven leader remained just beyond Henrietta's front gate. "I want the book," she demanded.

Initially, the impulse that struck Henrietta was to scream, "No." Her second response was a wish to destroy the volume. However, if she did not let them have it, they would keep coming back, and besides, her first priority now was to help Elgin.

Henrietta cuddled the lump that was her dog. As she cradled the little terrier in her arms, Elgin moaned and a muscle spasm contorted his small body. Henrietta rocked him, trying to give comfort.

A voice from out on the street screamed, "Give me the book!"

Henrietta wished *The Compleat Collectanea of Witchcraft & Demonology* was in her hands so she could hurl it at the witch. Heaven knew she did not want to be the guardian of it.

The front door banged again. For a second, Henrietta thought her mother had regained consciousness and come to see what all the commotion was about. But when the door swung wider, there was no one inside.

Another movement drew her attention, and Henrietta saw the dreaded volume the coven sought floating through the air onto the porch. It was enveloped in a shimmering silver fog, and rested on a small cloud composed of the same substance. The Compleat Collectanea paused near Henrietta, hovering a few feet above the wooden flooring. She wished she could just give the book to the witches and be rid of it.

No sooner did Henrietta think that, when the ancient volume righted on its small cloud. There was a churning in Henrietta's mid-section and light shot forth, focusing into a beam shining on the book.

The cover opened and light intensified, causing her eyes to water, yet she did not look away. Page after page turned, each of which was bathed in the brilliant spotlight. Flipping faster and faster until at last the end of the book was reached, and it closed.

"No!" shrilled the coven leader. "What have you done, you horrid girl?"

Henrietta turned and saw the woman collapse on the street, sobbing.

"You want the book," said Henrietta, "here it is."

"You've ruined it."

What happened next came as a surprise to Henrietta. Intuitively knowing what to do, she raised an arm toward the floating volume, and motioned at the coven leader lying on the pavement. As the book glided from the porch, Henrietta saw that it was no longer black with silver lettering. It now shined whitish, with golden letters.

Henrietta smiled when the witch leaped up and retreated from the volume as it approached her.

"No! Take it back..." The witch turned and fled down the roadway, shrieking, "Get away from me." But the hovering book pursued her around the corner and out of sight. Was the black cat fleeing with her Sylvester?

When Henrietta returned her attention to Elgin, his eyes opened and he wagged his tail. *'Served her right,'* said his thought voice in her mind.

Later that same week, Henrietta held Elgin on her lap when she sat on her front porch reading the newspaper that had been delivered earlier in the day. She read *The Atomizer Observer* headline:

Tornado Devastates Monmouth.

There was a picture of several buildings along Henrietta's street that were partly destroyed. Underneath the photo was a caption stating the damage had been to other parts of town as well, but no one had been seriously hurt, which was a miracle given the level of destruction.

One of the newspaper column sub-headings read:
Book Chases Woman Through Town.

There was a second photograph, but it was of the coven leader running for her life somewhere outside of Monmouth, with the book sailing along behind her on a freak wind. The photo credit listed the photographer as Hazel Harte.

"I wonder if that's *our* Hazel," said Henrietta.

Elgin did not answer with a thought voice. Instead, he snarled at the first picture and then snapped his teeth at the coven leader's image in the second.

Henrietta felt the same way, but she was too lady-like to growl and snap at a newspaper. At least not in public.

25: AFTERMATH

School was canceled for several days during the initial clean-up of the damaged portions of Monmouth. When Henrietta returned to the school after that, she found the playground had suffered much damage, and she stood there silently taking in the scene, trying to assess the extent of harm.

A huge pile of limbs and debris was stacked in one corner of the play area, and sectioned off with yellow, plastic, barricade tape proclaiming: "Danger- Do Not Enter."

Leaves and twigs littered the ground everywhere, and some of the school windows were covered-over by plywood, apparently waiting for the replacement of broken glass.

Henrietta thought this could not have resulted from her clash with the coven of witches, since the school was blocks from her home. Yet, the evidence before her was irrefutable. The effects of the tornado had indeed reached this far. She had mostly ignored looking at the damage to houses on her walk to school. She pretended not to see the new telephone and power poles put in to replace the downed and snapped-off ones from the storm. But now she had to face what had occurred, and the devastation she'd been a part of.

It was because of those awful witches, she thought. I would never do this on purpose. She started getting angry all over again about the coven. Especially when she noticed the damage done to the frame of the swing set, probably from a flying tree trunk. The swing nearest the dented area had been removed, undoubtedly because it was too low to the ground.

A scraping noise sounded just behind Henrietta, causing her to jump. Turning, she noticed several students stood silently behind her, also taking in the scene. Distress showed plainly on all of their faces. One third-grade boy, whose name Henrietta didn't know, scowled at the missing swing, and then looked at the damage to the school building. "My dad says they won't be able to use two first grade rooms for a couple of weeks at least."

A young, dark-haired girl, quite possibly a first-grader, nodded in agreement.

Henrietta gazed back at the pile in the corner. She thought of her neighbor's house—the one with part of its roof missing. That family had to stay in the motel over on highway 99 until insurance paid for the repairs. All the destruction the coven had caused came into Henrietta's mind, and her anger surged.

A little dust devil began in the open area between Henrietta and the stack of debris. It gathered momentum and increased in size, moving toward the pile, picking up twigs and leaves as it went along, and as her anger toward the coven continued, it magnified into a strong, twenty-foot-high whirlwind.

Behind Henrietta, a girl gasped.

What am I doing? Henrietta thought. It isn't the coven making *this* cyclone. It's me!

The swirling winds neared the accumulated debris and sucked up everything that was loose, funneling it high into the air. Bigger branches waved and thrashed about, and she thought that in another moment, if the tempest grew stronger, it might inhale the entire pile.

Fear gripped Henrietta. Why was she doing this? And what had she done the other day? It wasn't just the coven who created the tornado and mass devastation.

Perhaps Henrietta had done most of it, including chasing the witch down the street with the once-dreaded, but supposedly transformed book. Was the Compleat Collectanea really altered for the better? Why was this mini-tornado forming?

In desperation, Henrietta yelled, "Stop!"

The winds ceased and twigs and small stones plummeted to the earth, while leaves and papers fluttered slowly downward.

Initially relieved, Henrietta turned and saw the looks of shock on her schoolmates' faces. They stared at her without speaking. Apparently, they were more afraid of Henrietta than of the tornado.

"I didn't..." she began. But she knew that she had stopped it, and that she had also been its cause. Henrietta bolted from the playground, but as she fled, a familiar voice called from her right.

"Where are you going, Henrietta?" It was Allie.

Without turning, Henrietta yelled, "Home," as tears blurred her vision.

"Wait," Allie pleaded. The genuine caring in her voice almost caused Henrietta to halt, but she could not face anyone at the moment, and continued on.

"We're all scared," said Allie.

Henrietta faltered, but then shook her head, No, and stammered, "I can't..." and without looking at Allison, she ran even faster toward home.

She heard Jana asking Allison, "What's wrong with her?"

And the reply, "Probably just afraid...like the rest of us."

Henrietta was terribly upset. Not for the same reason as the other students, but from the devastation she'd caused in her own town.

More than anything else, what haunted her was the look in the eyes of that little first grade girl. A child who was more afraid of Henrietta than of the mini-tornado she'd just extinguished.

As Henrietta ran away, her hair flying in the wind, tears streaming down her cheeks and sobbing so loud she could hear little else, she sensed more than heard the worst thing of all.

The cackling sounds of a depraved witch rang in Henrietta's ears.

The vilest part was that she could not be sure if it was the coven leader, or someone much closer. A person so near that she could never get away from her.

Had Henrietta's sobbing turned into a cackle?

26: DEVIATION

Henrietta had started home with the intent of reversing the witch-hood she seemed to be developing. She did not know for certain if it was possible for her to undo that, but she had to try—whether her power came from black, or white magic. She wanted to be rid of it and had never wanted to be a witch in the first place. Whatever it took, she vowed to undo the strange power flowing through her.

She had only traveled one block away from school, however, when she remembered Mr. Baxter's pathetic physical state, and how the white light flowing out of her had reversed the crippling of his hands. She decided to do what she could to help him before permanently extinguishing her witchly powers.

Reversing her course, Henrietta headed for the teacher's house. She made good progress by running. Half a block from his dwelling, she heard the bark of his humongous dog, and something more.

"Slow down."

Henrietta glanced back to see Tabitha and Cory pursuing her. She stopped. It was no use. They would see her enter Mr. Baxter's house anyway. As she waited for them, she wondered how she had planned to get inside. She did not have a key like Tabitha did. Maybe it was good they'd followed. She wouldn't have to use her power to smash in his door, probably scaring him half to death.

Cory arrived first, out of breath. Tabitha came a moment later, also panting loudly.

"Good idea," she gasped, "checking on Mr. Baxter. We forgot all about him with the storm and everything."

Cory asked, "You think he's alright?"

Henrietta hadn't thought of that. "I hope so," she said, and ran toward his front door.

When they arrived, Tabitha pulled out the keys that hung on the string around her neck, and fumbled to undo the lock, her hands shook from the exertion of running.

"I've got asthma," she explained.

Inside the house, Tabitha yelled, "Mr. Baxter...are you okay?"

There was no answering voice, although the dog was making quite a ruckus out in the yard, and when they dashed into the bedroom, the smell in there was nauseous. The former teacher lay on the floor, breathing irregularly. There was a chilly breeze blowing in through the broken window and Mr. Baxter's lips were blue.

"Oh no," Cory cried. "What can we...?"

"Better call 911," said Tabitha, reaching into her pocket for her cell phone.

"No," said Henrietta. "There's something else I have to do first. Cory, go walk the dog or something to quiet him down. Tabitha...go watch the front door, and don't let anyone in until I tell you to."

Tabitha stared at her, phone raised, fingers poised to dial.

"Please," Henrietta, begged. "Do as I ask—both of you." She turned to Cory. "Now!"

He obeyed without comment, leaving the two girls alone with Mr. Baxter.

Tabitha continued staring, and finally said, "I want to watch what you do."

Henrietta felt the power welling up within her, as though the great need of the man lying on the floor called it forth. "Go lock the front door first," she said, giving her friend a gentle push in that direction.

The energy could no longer be contained. White light poured out of Henrietta, encircling Mr. Baxter, and then permeating his body, which glowed eerily. The familiar humming sound Henrietta heard when her talisman was working now churned through *her*.

The teacher before her writhed, then groaned, and parts of his body began transforming. His hands and fingers uncurled digit by digit, returning to normal. His spine and legs straightened and he appeared to regain his former height. His face became younger again. The light surrounding him flared even brighter, sending sparkling showers throughout the room, as if a giant Fourth of July fireworks had exploded indoors. Trash on the floor disappeared into the trashcan. The broken window instantly repaired itself as shattered glass leaped from the floor and reassembled, melding into a restored pane in its frame.

The bedroom's temperature heated up to a more comfortable seventy-degree range.

Finally, looking much more like his former self, Mr. Baxter lay peacefully on the floor; his breathing was normal. The light-energy softened, then gathered beneath him, and his body floated to three feet in the air, gliding sideways onto his remade bed. There was a smile on his face as he settled onto the comforter.

The churning within Henrietta ceased, and the illumination that had filled the room for a few minutes paled until the normal light level was restored. Only then did she wonder what had become of Tabitha.

Turning, Henrietta saw her friend slumped against the bedroom doorjamb. Surprisingly, there was no sign of horror on her face, no condemnation, but only wonder—and a wispy smile. "You did it," said Tabitha. "So...the rumors are true...and I think my asthma is also gone."

With that statement, Henrietta's own fears returned. "This is the last time," she said. "I'm done with magic...won't do it ever again."

"But why? You saved him."

"I wrecked everything else...especially my life." The vision of the little girl's fear-filled eyes invaded Henrietta's mind and she winced. Everyone would fear her now. Then she stopped thinking about that and realized what Tabitha had said. If she knew about the witch rumors, then she knew Henrietta was really Henrie. Thinking of the former Henrie, she moaned, "Oh."

Tabitha approached, placing her arm around her friend's shoulders. "He would have died if it weren't for you."

"He was that way because of my mother and the witches in her coven. They want me to be like them. But I won't. They will do anything to turn me evil."

"We won't let them," Tabitha gave her a hug.

Henrietta sank to the floor, sobbing. Between sniffles, as Tabitha held and rocked her, Henrietta told her friend the story of sleeping out in the tool shed with her dog, and described all the evil spells her mother had placed around their house. She talked of the awful coven, especially its leader, and the hateful black book.

The last part that she related was about her facing the coven, which had gathered across the street from her house, and the terrible storm generated over their heads. How Henrietta hated them and accidentally did what the coven wanted, causing the light on her side of the street to intensify the winds, increasing the destructive tornado.

"But none of that is *your* fault," said Tabitha.

Cory burst through the bedroom entryway. "The front door is locked, so I had to go back around to get in, after I.... What happened?"

"The medics were already here and left," said Tabitha. "They gave Mr. Baxter a shot, and he's much better now."

Henrietta couldn't help smiling as Cory looked about the room in bewilderment, and saw the fully-restored teacher lying there—then he eyed the spruced-up bed chamber and the like-new window.

"Right," he said softly. "That was *some injection.*"

Both girls giggled at him, but then they could not stop, and collapsed onto the floor in a laughing fit.

27: MORE DIARY

Henrietta retrieved Delvettica's diary from the bathroom linen closet, and slipped it under the back of her shirt before returning to the hall. The plan was to sneak upstairs and inside her room before her mother knew she was home.

Delvettica hummed happily in the kitchen as her daughter swung open the door to the upstairs, which squeaked loudly.

"Is that you, Henrietta?"

Elgin barked from the kitchen, and came trotting gaily into the hallway.

Henrietta thought how happy her mother sounded. She's not screaming at me lately, and doesn't call me Henrie anymore. Plus, Elgin goes voluntarily in the kitchen with her. It is all just so weird—but good.

Henrietta answered, "I've got lots of homework."

"Dinner will be ready at five, dear."

"Okay."

Elgin bounced up the stairs behind Henrietta, who kept shaking her head. She could not believe her mom's behavior lately. Especially the great meals she made. Henrietta also could not believe how Tabitha and the others had rallied around her to squelch rumors about the mini-tornado which had formed on the playground, until Henrietta stopped it.

Tabitha also convinced her that the coven might return some day, and if that happened, Henrietta would need her powers to keep the witches from harming her, and probably her mother and Elgin, as well.

Henrietta removed the diary and held onto it as she climbed up on her bed, bouncing up and down. Elgin watched from the floor in the center of her room. Lately, he did not often talk to her with his thought words.

Her lighthearted moment vanished when she sat down on her checkerboard comforter, with Elgin curled beside her leg, and opened her mother's journal at a random page well past the middle.

It was noticeable how the cursive seemed more distorted the farther into the diary Henrietta read. The change in her mother's thinking was clear in the later entries. At first, she had been full of curiosity about witches. Then she'd been repulsed.

Over time, however, the mental torture of the coven had its desired effects. Delvettica came to hate everyone not in the coven, and to cast ever-darker spells on most of the people around her. Eventually, that included Henrietta's grandmother.

The now-opened entry was written in an angry, scrawled hand, which Henrietta read silently.

Kynthia is furious with me at Henrie's slow progress. She says by now Henrie should be casting spells against her classmates and wanting to join our coven. Ours should be the most powerful sisterhood of witches on the west coast.

No matter what I do, how many spells I cast on her favorite belongings or her ratty little dog, Henrie resists my will. Of course, I realize now that the method my mother used to lure me into the coven does not work on my daughter. She's not power hungry the way I was. We need some new way to influence Henrie. Why can't Kynthia realize that?

Of course, there is the very real possibility Kynthia plans to destroy me after Henrie's conversion, just as her mother sacrificed mine. I hated my mom so much by then, I laughed while they murdered her, and gloried in her painful demise—which brought our coven's power to a new, much higher level.

Perhaps our two bloods, Henrie's and mine, will flow together on the altar stone, because Kynthia is losing her patience. She may decide to sacrifice us both. Even though she wants Henrie in the coven more than anything I can remember, she is afraid of what will happen if we can't turn her. Will Henrie go over to the other side? Perhaps. If she does, and we are sacrificed, it will be a glorious ending for...

There, Delvettica's words stopped, and Henrietta gazed at a newspaper clipping pasted into the diary. It was an article from the Sunday Oregamian. An imposing photo topped the clipping; the picture of a

Stonehenge replica built on the Washington side of the Columbia River. The text noted this latter-day American version was now more complete than the original Stonehenge situated for centuries on England's Salisbury Plain.

Since that one had been robbed of so many of its great stones over the years, the American facsimile was in some ways superior. It had been constructed by a turn of the century pacific northwest road builder just a mile or so from his imposing Maryhill Castle, overlooking the broad, majestic Columbia River. The Stonehenge replica was aligned so accurately, and it was so identical to the original, that scientists studied its relationship to the cosmos.

This news article, as Henrietta read further, was actually about witchcraft and the threat it posed to innocent children. A Seattle therapist who specialized in treating Satanic Ritualistic Abuse survivors gave a sketchy account of the gruesome details, and referenced yearly sacrificial dates marked on the satanic calendar. Even though the description of forcing children to watch a human body being dismembered was brief, it became repulsively etched in Henrietta's mind.

Looking again at the large, flat stone lying surrounded by the megalithic circle near the center of the photograph, Henrietta began to wonder. Had her grandmother perished on that benign-appearing hunk of rock?

Was that where the diary entry suggested she and her mother might also be sacrificed?

Glancing back above the news clipping at her mother's scrawled writing, Henrietta whispered, "Kynthia must be the coven's leader."

Elgin whimpered in his sleep as Henrietta realized she had not discovered the cult leader's name on any previous diary pages. There had seemed to be some prohibition against writing it–even in her mother's diary. Perhaps the witches were not supposed to speak it aloud, either.

28: THE VISITOR

A creaking sound alerted Henrietta that her mother was climbing the steps to the upstairs bedroom. Henrietta closed the diary and slipped it under her pillow, then sat up on her bed.

The door opened, but still Elgin did not awaken to greet their unseen visitor. When a shadowed figure moved across the threshold, Henrietta's mother seemed transformed, she looked so much younger.

It took a moment for Henrietta to realize the dark form of the woman standing there was not her mother. So convinced had she been about who would enter, she felt disoriented knowing it was someone else—an entirely unexpected presence.

"Kynthia!" The name escaped Henrietta's lips.

The witch wore flowing black pants, somewhat like culottes, only much longer, and a matching top, probably silk, with medieval-appearing sleeves that draped into elongated, flared oval openings below her hands.

The coven leader grinned. It was not a reassuring gesture, to be sure. Her face was the one Henrietta had glimpsed once before, the pretty, youthful visage usually hidden beneath the uglier middle layer of deception.

What, if anything, rested beneath that one? Henrietta wondered, knowing this comelier countenance represented even more evil than the others.

The witch moved across the room and sat on the foot of the bed, uncomfortably close to the surprised girl. Still, the little Scotty did not waken, but instead he commenced snoring. The coven leader smirked maliciously at his sleeping form.

Henrietta placed her arm protectively over him. What she wanted to do was snatch her dog up, leap off the bed, and flee the room, but she seemed powerless to act.

"Now you are one of us," said the witch.

That assertion stunned Henrietta. She wanted to yell a strong denial back, but managed only a pathetic, "No."

A sneer accompanied the woman's next words. "Who speaks my name is one with us, a coven member. No other persons may utter it. You have taken the plunge at last, ripped away any remaining barriers."

Henrietta's next protest was even weaker than the first, as tears trickled down her face.

"And to seal the bargain, we will sacrifice your little mutt. Actually, *you* will sacrifice him. He will not waken to feel a thing."

Kynthia reached under the ample fabric of her left sleeve and withdrew a row of tiny, three-inch-long spears. The black steel points accounted for half their length, and were attached to the ends of dark metal shafts. They frightened Henrietta all out of proportion to their size.

Swallowing hard, she tried to look away, but could not. The thirteen small weapons were attached together by a transparent strip holding them in a neat row. Their shafts reposed in miniscule cylinders of the same clear material that kept the lances evenly spaced along the base strip.

Kynthia withdrew a spear at one end and held it up for observation.

"Razor sharp," she explained. "He won't feel a thing."

The witch held the point just above the skin of her exposed wrist, and drew it in a suggestive line. "We'll do you first," she said, "to show it isn't painful."

Henrietta shrunk back.

A chuckle was the witch's only reply. Watching Henrietta's shaken response to the lances, Kynthia lifted the point up to her own neck and jabbed it beneath the skin, smiling as she did so. "Doesn't hurt a bit," she said as she moved the same blade toward Henrietta's neck. "You'll see."

Eyes open wide as she saw the flow of blood down Kynthia's skin, Henrietta tried to swallow but could not. Is this how it is to be done, she wondered, small sharp jabs until I bleed to death right here on my quilt, in my own bedroom?

Apparently, there would be no stone-top sacrifice for Henrietta.

Elgin made a barking sound in his sleep. His little legs ran, but he was now on his side so that his two lower paws ineffectually grazed the fabric.

In that moment when the witch's mesmerizing eyes looked down at the terrier, Henrietta's mind raced freely. The witch would kill her here on the bed, if not frighten her into joining the coven. One desperate hope rose in Henrietta. Perhaps the witch could be made to take her own life.

Envisioning Kynthia plunging the lance deep in her own throat, Henrietta thought she felt the churning of energy in her midsection. But it was different than before, and as she looked at the witch's neck, there was a dark cloud forming there. Henrietta saw a twinkle of joy in those beautiful but deceptive eyes and the trace of a sly smile on Kynthia's lips.

This was another trick to get Henrietta to use black magic, and it had almost worked. Feeling her anger rising at being so easily duped, Henrietta recalled how she had met the force of the coven's black storm with white light. She also remembered that clash of opposing powers had resulted in a devastating tornado. Plus, there was the overheard statement of this vile coven leader deep in the sub-basements: "With her hatred, we will control her."

Another awareness also surfaced. It felt as though a giant dark hand gripped Henrietta. That grasp was connected to something not present in her bed chamber. She sensed the rest of the coven gathered across the street, inside a makeshift pentagram of black ribbons positioned on the ground. The witches chanted, but there was more—much more.

A symbol held by the center-most witch was a focal point for other covens who were also assembled in their distant pentagrams, all linked together to reinforce Kynthia. Henrietta noticed an identical black metal symbol in the folds of the cult leader's top. It rang with the combined energies of all the covens, and drew to it, along with their evil vibrations, the most vile of spirits from the darkest underworlds. Her nostrils filled with the awful stench.

Henrietta's horror was so great, she could no longer breath. She stood no chance against this wicked assemblage.

"Ah-ha." A lighthearted laugh came from the corner of the room.

Henrietta looked over to see Hazel standing there, apparently without a care in the world. She leaned on a folded-up umbrella.

"I thought you girls knew when you were beaten, and had gone home to plot each other's destruction," Hazel said to the coven leader.

Kynthia's head swirled around. "Who are *you?*"

"Just a friend."

"You're not my friend." There was no longer a smile on the coven leader's face as she rose from the foot of Henrietta's bed.

Hazel chuckled. "Well dear, right now I'm the closest thing you've got to a friend. You are about ten seconds away from self-destruction."

"You are a white magician?" Kynthia asked.

Hazel shook her head. "I'm not into *your* world of magic at all, dear. Now pay attention and you might survive. You might even learn something."

Kynthia tried to scoff, but Henrietta could tell she was spooked as she looked around, trying to figure out how Hazel had entered the room. The window was shut, and it would have been noticeable if she'd crossed from the doorway. Surely, Hazel hadn't hid in the closet. Henrietta could almost read the witch's mind as she tried to make sense of the situation.

Henrietta was used to Hazel showing up unexpectedly, and took a deep breath of relief, pulling Elgin onto her lap. In her mid-section, she felt the churning of energy. It was strong like when she'd helped Mr. Baxter get well. With the thought about him, Henrietta realized these witches were also sick, but in a different way. She let the healing energy fill her body, and watched as the light flowed out around her.

Kynthia's mouth dropped open when her eyes returned to view Henrietta after surveying the room. "Ach..."

Something within Kynthia reacted so strongly to viewing the white radiance as to cause Henrietta to jolt backwards off the bed like she'd been hit with a high-voltage current from a downed power line. That same force flung Kynthia clear across the room.

The brilliance around Henrietta intensified even more.

Kynthia looked toward the door, obviously about to bolt in that direction.

"Chill," said Hazel. "You need a little vacation, dear. Somewhere you can cool down."

The coven leader was there in the room one second–and gone the next.

Henrietta still saw in her memory the shocked look on Kynthia's face just before she disappeared.

"I don't know when those silly girls will learn," said Hazel. "Are you all right, dear?"

She walked to Henrietta after securing the top crook of her umbrella in the elbow joint of her left arm, and placed her other arm reassuringly around the girl's shoulder. Hazel was seemingly unaffected by the ball of energy that now formed a cocoon around Henrietta.

Nodding, she likewise put an arm around Hazel in a return gesture of thanks. "Is my mom okay?"

"Heavens, yes...she's better than ever. You freed her from their dark ways. She's in the kitchen baking you a pie, and she threw out all the herbs that aren't for cooking or healing."

Hazel looked up for a moment, and then said, "Silly me. I nearly forgot about that other poor, misguided girl. Let's see if she's cooled off yet."

There was a large hologram image projected at the center of the bedroom and Henrietta saw the coven leader shivering in the interior of an industrial meat locker. She hung from a large metal hook for hanging the meat.

In the blink of an eye, a very different Kynthia now appeared in the center of the room. Her clothing was dusted with white flecks, and her teeth were chattering as she hugged herself for warmth. The frost on her face, especially on her eyebrows and eyelids, gave her a whole new appearance. Her facial features were not those of any of the three visages Henrietta had witnessed before. She looked, even with her snowy appearance, more human. An actual icicle dangled from the tip of her nose.

The half-frozen witch stomped her feet as if trying to return life to them.

"Run along now, dear," said Hazel.

Kynthia did not wait for a second urging, but stumbled toward the door.

"Oh, by the way," Hazel added, "if any of you visit this girl again with ill intent, you and they will be on permanent holiday in a place similar to the one you just visited. Now be gone."

Kynthia bolted forward, but disappeared before reaching the doorway. She left a white sprinkling, like powdered sugar, on the surface of the rug. The frosty traces were already converting into drops of water.

Hazel noted the puzzled look on Henrietta's face and said with a chuckle, "She has just dropped in on her little group of friends."

Henrietta could hear women screaming frantically from clear across the street.

"I think their little meeting has just adjourned," Hazel commented. "Now, let's go down and see if your mother will share some of her wonderful herb tea. I've been looking forward to meeting her—officially.

29: A CURIOUS MEETING

For a plump woman who appeared to be in her mid-fifties, Hazel moved down Henrietta's staircase in a sprightly manner. But when she smiled a greeting at Delvettica upon entering the kitchen, her face seemed more like a woman in her thirties.

Henrietta would have marveled about that, except she was preoccupied with the disappearance of the umbrella that had been hanging from Hazel's left arm. Even that did not occupy Henrietta's thoughts for long, as she observed the meeting between Hazel and her mother.

Delvettica took it as perfectly natural when a woman she could not accurately remember seeing before entered her kitchen from the interior of the house and introduced herself.

"I'm Hazel, a friend of your daughter's. I'm so pleased to *really* meet you at last, Delvettica."

Henrietta's mother wiped the flour from her hands onto her apron. "You seem so familiar, Hazel, but I don't quite remember...."

Seeing white traces still clinging to her skin, she turned toward the sink to wash off the remnants.

"Oh, nonsense," said Hazel, extending her right hand, "what's a little flour between friends?"

As the two laughed and shook hands, Henrietta could not help but notice how youthful and even pretty her mother appeared. The hideous wart was gone from her nose, and other facial features had softened, giving her the blush of near-youth.

"Could I trouble you for a cup of that wonderful-smelling mint tea?" asked Hazel.

Delvettica warned, "There's a pinch of nettle in it, as well."

"Perfect...just how I like it, and so good for a body...plus, it's more full-flavored, and delicious that way."

Henrietta watched in wonder as the two sat at the kitchen table, sipping herbal tea like old friends, and chatting away.

"The pie should be cooled down enough by now," said Delvettica. Without looking away from Hazel she added, "Henrietta, will you cut us each a slice?"

Would she ever. The Marion berry pie was done to perfection. She dished the first piece onto a dessert plate—after she'd quickly scrubbed it clean, of course. That saucer had not seen the light of day for years. Henrietta smelled the steamy aroma, and watched luscious juice flow out of the pie onto the china.

"There's ice cream in the freezer," said her mother.

Henrietta ladled large scoops of old-fashioned French vanilla onto the warm pieces of pie, and watched it begin to soften and run into tiny white rivulets, flowing around the berry dessert to form into a small, sweet mote.

But the best part was when Henrietta sat across from Hazel and her mom and lifted the first bite toward her lips. The flavors from the pie crust, vine-ripened berries, and French vanilla all melted together into one glorious taste inside her mouth. "Mmm!"

"Eat all you want, Henrietta, there's another pie cooling over there."

Henrietta could not believe her eyes. She stared at a second one resting on an elevated pie rack beside the kitchen window, and then her eyes closed and she lost herself in the flavor of warm berry pie mixed with ice cream. If she was dreaming, she didn't ever want to wake up.

"Truly delicious," Hazel said after she had swallowed her first bite.

"By the way, Delvettica, do you think Henrietta could visit me at my place in the country on Saturday? I have a horse that really needs to be ridden—a gentle mare."

Delvettica looked questioningly at her daughter.

Henrietta's mouth was still full of her second bite of dessert.

"Oh, you don't have to answer right now," said Hazel. "I know you're still chewing."

That wasn't totally accurate. Henrietta was fully savoring and immersing herself in the delectable flavors.

She had never ridden a horse. Never even had the opportunity, since she didn't own one and no kids that she'd known over the years who did have horses had ever been her friends. She'd always wanted to go horseback riding, but now when the opportunity arose, she was a little bit scared. What if she got bucked off, or the horse stepped on her foot, or bit her. Those were all things Henrietta had heard about.

As though she'd read Henrietta's mind, Hazel said, "She's a very gentle mare, no bad habits, and she loves kids. My grandchildren used to ride her, but now they like horses with more spirit, and they have ones of their own."

Henrietta nodded, not wanting to swallow prematurely and choke. Plus, she was concerned she might scream her reply–"YES"–so loudly, the sound would carry out into the yard, filling the neighborhood, and be heard in adjacent homes.

"You might like to come as well," said Hazel to Delvettica. "I have an herb garden where you'd likely see something you'd need a start of. There's watercress growing in the stream, too." Looking at Henrietta, she added, "And pollywogs to catch in the pond."

A pond with pollywogs and maybe fish? Henrietta could barely wait.

"I'd love to see your herbs," said Delvettica, "and I bet Henrietta would like to go horseback riding, although she's never ridden before. Except...we don't have a car."

"Then it's all settled, I will transport you, and this will be her first horseback ride."

Hazel winked at Henrietta, who smiled in return. She hadn't learned to wink yet—never had the opportunity. Actually, she'd had little occasion to do much of anything but hide in the tool shed with Elgin and be a loner at school, until this last week or so.

Things were changing fast.

30: BACK AT SCHOOL

The playground was full of kids behaving as if nothing had ever happened to close their school. The debris had mostly been hauled away, and all of the broken windows had been replaced. Henrietta walked toward the building to see if she could find Tabitha, but Allie called out to her.

"Hey, wait up."

Turning, Henrietta saw Allie and Janna approach. They were not alone, Adelle was with them.

"Why'd you ditch Adelle?" Janna asked in a mean voice.

Henrietta said, looking at the supposedly aggrieved girl, "I didn't. Did I?"

"You and Tabitha went to Mr. Baxter's without her," Allie said.

Cory arrived just then. "Adelle, where were you yesterday? We looked all over for you."

"You did?" Adelle asked, then looked at Janna suspiciously. "I was with Allie and Janna, and they said—"

"That's old news now," said Allie. "We were worried...thought something happened to you,

Henrietta. Why'd you run away from school yesterday?"

"Her mom was sick," said Cory.

Janna said, "Again? What's wrong with her? She's always ill."

"She's better now," said Henrietta.

Allie moved away from the group. "Come on. Let's play wall ball."

Henrietta realized Allie was diverting attention away from herself and the situation she'd tried to orchestrate. Henrietta soon stood in the wall ball line, awaiting her turn. She'd purposely slowed so she would be at the end of the queue. Her gaze periodically swept the play area in search of Tabitha, because out of all the kids, Tabitha was her *real* friend–compared to Allie and Janna, anyway.

Cory seemed pretty nice, especially now, when he'd come to her rescue. Adelle was okay, friendly most times, but it put Henrietta off, the irritable bowel thing. As she thought about the girl's malady, she wondered if she could help Adelle the way she had aided Mr. Baxter.

"Hi-ya."

Henrietta turned and saw Tabitha in line just behind her. Somehow, her friend had approached without Henrietta spotting her. "Hey."

The girls hugged briefly. Tabitha leaned her head forward just for a second and whispered, "Mr. Baxter is going to come back to school."

"When?"

"You heard that Mrs. Fern is expecting a baby, right? Well, he's going to take over her class as the substitute when she's on maternity leave. Since he was disabled, they hired Miss Winsom to take his class."

"That's great," Henrietta said. "Him coming back."

The ball came bouncing their way, and Tabitha slipped in front to retrieve it, tossing it back to Janna.

"You missed," said Allie, "so you're out."

"Did not," Janna replied. "You're out for doing cross-country. Nobody could get that one."

"Do over," said Allie.

Janna wasn't happy, but she obviously didn't want to get in a fight with her best friend, maybe her only friend.

A playground attendant blew her whistle and said, "Allie, you're out."

Allie turned on the woman, about to say something cutting, at least that's how it looked to Henrietta, but then Allie thought better of it.

"Just a stupid game, anyway." She stomped to the back of the line behind Tabitha.

Janna tossed the ball to Adelle, who was at the front of the line, and mimicked Allie as she stomped off to join her friend.

"Stupid teachers," Janna said just loud enough so the girls near her would overhear, but too softly for the adult to catch. "They can't see anything. Why doesn't she go find kids doing something really wrong and leave us alone."

"Yeah," agreed Allie. Then she turned so she could see Henrietta's face and asked, "If your mom's better, why don't you come over to my house tonight?"

Henrietta sensed this was probably a trap. After everything she'd experienced with the coven, she was extra alert to any deceit at school, especially from the dragon twins. "Uh–"

Tabitha interrupted, "We're all going over to see Mr. Baxter after school. Would you and Janna like to come along? He's feeling lots better."

Henrietta could see that Allie felt caught in her own snare. No way was she going to hang out with her nemesis, Tabitha.

"Mom's fixing something special," Allie said. "Gotta go straight home."

Henrietta was so tired of the wicked games so many people played, she started to become angry. What plan was Allie hatching now? Some form of divide and conquer, most likely. As Henrietta's feelings grew, she felt a churning in her gut, but not the kind that resulted in light-energy. Still staring at Allie, she saw a dark cloud forming around this girl who often pretended to be her friend.

Scared, Henrietta made a conscious effort to change her thoughts. She asked, "Could you come over after you eat the treat your mom is making for you? We'd really like you to see how Mr. Baxter is doing."

The surprising thing to Henrietta was that she really meant it. She did not know why, but more words popped out of her. "If you want to, after that, we could *all* go to my house. Tabitha and you guys...Cory, Adelle–everybody. My mom made pies, and there's still one left. The best Marion berry pie you ever tasted."

That offer got Allie's attention. "Real homemade?"

"Yep! And we got some great French vanilla ice cream to go with it." She hoped there was still enough left. If everyone came, that would be six kids, including Henrietta.

"I'll call my mom right after school and ask," said Allie.

Henrietta knew it was a done deal.

31: TEACHER'S HOUSE

Henrietta and her group of friends waited on the porch for Mr. Baxter to answer his doorbell. Even Tabitha was getting nervous about how long it took him. Henrietta wondered if he was really better, or if he'd had a relapse.

"Waiting for me?"

They all jumped.

Henrietta swiveled around to see Mr. Baxter with his mastiff-crossbred dog, Duke, tugging at the end of a leash.

"I took him for a little walk," he said, "right after his bath. To give him a chance to dry off before he could roll in the dirt."

The big dog's fur glistened in the sun. His coat looked more brindled than when Henrietta had seen him before, and the short hairs of his muzzle now looked jet black.

"He's beautiful," said Henrietta. She patted her hand on her leg and Duke lurched forward to greet her, dragging Mr. Baxter nearly three feet.

Allie leaped back behind some of the others with a little yelp.

"He's big enough to ride," Janna said, also shifting away.

Mr. Baxter said, "I'll put him in the yard."

"Can't we play with him?" Cory protested.

Henrietta thought Mr. Baxter looked exactly like his old self from the year before, as if there had never been anything wrong with him.

But in the time it took her to notice that, Duke nosed Henrietta off the porch and the two of them rolled around on the lawn.

"I thought we came here to see—" Allie began, but Duke stopped play-mauling Henrietta, tilted his head toward the porch and gave a look that shut Allie up.

Mr. Baxter coiled the dog leash and bounded up the steps.

"Come on in you guys. I think I've got some hot chocolate somewhere. No telling how old it is, but I don't think it ever goes bad if the lid is closed."

"Come, Duke," he called as he unlocked the door.

Allie and Janna had made their way into positions half-hidden behind the others, and were nearest the door, so they bolted inside to avoid the dog.

Mr. Baxter waited at the entranceway for Henrietta and Duke. As the playful brute crossed the threshold, his master said, "House rules, Duke."

To Henrietta's surprise, the dog seemed to calm right down.

"If he doesn't behave, he knows I'll put him out in the yard."

When Henrietta entered the house, she saw Duke curled up on a giant dog pillow she had not noticed before.

All the living room curtains were open and she observed a number of things she'd overlooked previously. Most obvious was the layer of dust on most everything. Duke had left a meandering trail of giant paw prints across the hardwood floor to his bed.

"I'm having a cleaning service come in tomorrow and spruce this place up."

As if that was their cue to cleanse things, Tabitha pulled the vacuum from the back of the coat closet, and undid the cord.

"Whoa there," said Mr. Baxter. "You kids have done way more than your share of keeping this place clean. Right now it's chocolate time.

Henrietta noticed that Allie and Janna looked relieved, and were the first to follow him into the kitchen. Henrietta was last.

Duke did not want to be abandoned and leaped off his overstuffed cushion to force his way past her.

Then, to make up for that, he licked her hand and leaned against her as Mr. Baxter prepared the cocoa. When Duke sat down, he was nearly as tall as Henrietta.

"So...how have things been going at school?" Mr. Baxter asked, and the others all started talking at once, except for Henrietta, of course.

She was too busy enjoying the moment with her friends, and feeling good about the reversal of misfortune for her favorite teacher.

She gave Duke a hug around his massive neck.

32: FIRST PARTY

It was a totally new experience for Henrietta, being the leader of a parade of six jabbering children up Broad Street towards her house.

She had to remind herself this was not a dream.

Allie had loaned her cell phone to Henrietta to call and confirm with Delvettica that the whole gang could come over.

When they got to the wrought iron gate, Henrietta was thankful there were no longer ritualistic symbols in its decorative design. That reminded her of the rumors all the kids had mocked her about—her mother being a witch, and all that. There had not been a single mean word from her classmates recently, and none from her friends as they stood before *the house.*

It was totally silent behind Henrietta, however, until she pushed open her front gate. The noise was not so much from the screech of the metal as it was from Elgin's barking. The small Scottish terrier was overjoyed to see they had company.

He burst forth through the opening and cavorted about between the children, leaping up on their legs.

He did not curtail his questionable behaviors as he usually did when Henrietta reprimanded him, but continued his wild antics.

Because of the reaction to Duke, Henrietta was unprepared for Allie's response when she squealed and leaned over to pick the small dog up.

"What a cute puppy. You're so lucky Henrietta... my mom won't let me have one. What's his name?"

"Elgin."

To Henrietta's surprise, the small terrier calmed right down, except for his tail, which continued to flit back and forth on high wag from under Allie's encircling arms.

"He's heavier than he looks," Allie said.

Henrietta led the way through the front door and into her house. She dropped her backpack on a bench in the foyer and the others followed her example. By the time the line of kids entered the living room, they could easily detect the aroma from cooking desserts.

"Mm...your house smells good," said Adelle. "I wish my mom baked."

There was shoving from behind as the group proceeded down the hallway leading to the kitchen. Each step of the way, Henrietta could not help noting how clean and orderly her home now appeared. The light streaming in through the living room windows was simply dazzling, but that did not prepare her for the illumination in the kitchen.

There were no herb sacks hanging from the ceiling to blemish the view or to cast scary shadows across the floor. The drain board was lined with freshly baked pies and pastries.

Delvettica was downright radiant, even with a spot of white flour on her almost normal-sized nose and white hand-prints on her apron. "I'm so glad you could bring your friends over."

Henrietta felt a sudden worry. This fairy-tale life she was in could not continue. At some point, it must come crashing down around her.

"It smells wonderful in here, Mrs. House," said Tabitha.

The others quickly agreed, "Yes!"

And before Henrietta knew it, her friends were all seated around the kitchen table, which had been pulled out from the wall for this occasion. With the addition of the card table covered with a fancy cloth, there was room for everybody.

Delvettica commenced cutting large pieces of pie she placed on actual plates, not paper imitations, and asked, "Who wants ice cream?"

The "Me's" were universal.

Henrietta operated the ice cream scooper, and Tabitha delivered the slices of pie a la mode to the others, saying, "Who wants berry," and "Who wants apple."

Allie continued to snuggle Elgin in her lap even as she sat in her chair at the table, and to Henrietta's surprise, he remained mannerly throughout their mealtime. He didn't try even once to lick the forkfuls of dessert passing by on the way to Allie's mouth.

Janna, who had been unusually quiet since entering Henrietta's house, whispered something Henrietta could not hear.

"What?" she asked.

"I wish my mom was like this," Janna repeated louder, and since everyone had gone silent the moment before, those words echoed for all to hear.

"Well, dear," said Mrs. House, "most moms have to work now-a-days, and they don't have time for baking and such."

"Not mine," said Janna. "She's an alcoholic. All she does is sit at home and drink."

In the silence that followed, Henrietta realized how little she knew about her friends' home lives. Was having a mother delving into the black arts any worse than having an alcoholic parent? She did not know for certain.

Allie put down her fork and hugged Elgin. "My mom is always in a hurry, and even when she's home, she's either on the phone or using her laptop, to sell real estate."

No one could remain gloomy for long, though, since Mrs. House just kept dishing more pie, and when the kids were so stuffed they could not eat one more bite, she declared, "It's time for charades. Everyone in the living room. Just leave your dishes right where they are. I'll clean up later."

Henrietta didn't know how to play charades, or pretty much any other games. Not even common board games. It turned out that none of her friends knew how to play charades either.

But they all had fun learning.

33: LAST ENTRY

Long after her friends had left, Henrietta sat on her bed with Elgin curled beside her. In her lap she held her mother's diary. She had read most of the way through the journal on previous occasions, but this time the small book opened near the very end, seemingly of its own accord.

Henrietta found the entry on that page was much different than previous ones.

That awful talisman is undoing everything. If this keeps up, we will lose Henrietta for good, and I was so close to turning her. Why didn't I listen to my mother? She warned me not to open that box with its dreadful clothespin. Why was the amulet handed down through my family, anyway—why wasn't it demolished? And, why didn't I destroy it?

Henrietta thought that it was probably for the same reason the five witches ahead of her mother could not destroy it. They all had at least some white magic in them.

That is why Delvettica, fearing her own temptations, told her daughter to hide her talisman. She could not bring herself to annihilate it.

But instead, Henrietta had used it to undo all the terrible hexes she could find.

Henrietta had likewise discovered her family's awfullest, most unforgivable secret. Most families had **dark secrets**, but hers was a secret of *light*. Somewhere in the previous untold generations, one of her great, great, something-or-other witch ancestors had done the unthinkable, dabbled in white magic.

It must only have been by accident that Delvettica learned the true nature of the talisman. Who would suspect such an unlikely object as a wooden clothespin of corrupting her ancestors and passing on the white magic?

Henrietta pulled up the coarse string with the amulet at its end, and studied the surface markings. Most of the small figures etched into the variegated wood-grain represented a witch who'd embraced the light.

There were many generations of white witches in that unbroken line. They marched down through the years across one face of the clothespin, then crossed over and went up the other side. She saw that each figure was lighter in color than the previous one, until the six just before Henrietta. In those last few, the light had nearly vanished.

Goosebumps now covered Henrietta's arms, and shivers coursed through her body because she saw what her true heritage had always been. The talisman was a testament to her inner abilities and a record of those white witches who'd preceded her—much more than it was a powerful amulet. In that respect, Hazel had been correct.

Closely studying the line of witches, Henrietta realized that one of the figures near the end was her grandmother who'd been sacrificed.

That form was light at the feet, but darker through the torso, and black at her head, yet the line had continued unbroken. As Henrietta watched with fascination, the carving that resembled her mother lightened in color. How did that happen?

In front of Delvettica was a small star etched into the wood. That tiny star suddenly transformed into a girl of light. Somehow, the amulet recorded each new generation even without a woodcarver's handiwork.

Closing her eyes, Henrietta concentrated on the middle of her body and felt the familiar churning energy. Instantly, light filled her entire being and radiated out in all directions, brightening her room and passing on through the walls. She wondered how far such light could travel and what transformations it would perform wherever it went.

Focusing on that radiance, Henrietta found she could accompany it and witness the effects on everything it passed through. In consciousness, Henrietta flowed forth and viewed the outside of her house. It now glowed white as though it had just been painted. The foliage in her yard seemed brighter, and even the old backyard shed appeared new.

Curious to see what her mother was up to, Henrietta shifted attention to the visible light permeating down through her house. Following the radiance, she found her mom bustling about in the kitchen, humming as she cleaned up.

While Mrs. House pulled the soiled cloth off the table, Henrietta focused on the dirty dishes in the sink and in an instant they were sparkling clean. The entire room began to glow.

Boy, was this going to make housework a breeze.

Concentrating back toward her bedroom, she saw Elgin still sleeping beside her. On a whim, she followed the radiance from her body, traveling at another angle through the floor, downward into the basement and then onward to the subbasements.

There, she encountered the hexing room with its pentagram on the see-through floor. Gazing intently at the symbol of sorcery, she saw it glow white and then disappear.

There were distant screams when that occurred. The building shuddered and then everything silenced. Peace had at last descended upon her home.

Henrietta opened her eyes and sighed. She was back on her bed.

All was well in her world.

34: NEW BEGINNING

During the next school day, Henrietta found that a new drama had surfaced between her two groups of friends. Allie and Janna were in one "camp," against Tabitha, Cory and Adelle in the other. Both groups wanted her to be on *their* side—linked against her other friends. She managed not to do that, but nearly ended up with both groups disliking her.

Relations were so frosty by the day's end, that no one invited Henrietta to their home, or to visit Mr. Baxter. And for certain, nobody asked if they could accompany *her* home. Which was a shame because Henrietta guessed her mother had again baked pies and other goodies.

During the most trying moments of that day's peer squabbles, Henrietta briefly considered the idea of using magic to "fix" things. Each time such thoughts arose, she remembered Cory with a black fog on his back, screaming and holding his ankle. Then she heard Hazel's warning repeat in her mind, "Your own unhelpful decisions can lead you down the wrong path more quickly than an entire coven of evil witches."

Henrietta thought about these things as she walked home alone. Once there, she went quietly through the front door, and although she smelled something chocolatey and delicious baking in the kitchen, she slipped upstairs without talking to her mother.

She felt guilty about Elgin until she saw him curled up on her bed, his little tail wagging a greeting. Henrietta sat down and pulled him onto her lap, rocking back and forth with him. "You are my bestest friend in the whole world," she told him.

Elgin licked her face.

He soon deserted her, however, and Henrietta decided he'd gone down to the kitchen to mooch some doggie treats from her mom. Henrietta was tempted to do the same thing—but not for dog treats, of course.

Instead, she decided there were some things she really needed to sort out first. As she lay back on her pillow and reflected on her day at school, the worst part of that experience wasn't surviving the drama created by the other kids.

Although, thinking about the manipulations of some of her friends, she almost wished she was plain old Henrie again, and didn't have to deal with it all.

Taking a deep sigh, Henrietta knew the fears about witch covens waiting to snag her into their ranks no longer bothered her. The most disturbing thing was that Henrietta herself was her only real enemy.

An apprehensive twinge shuddered through Henrietta. Was that sound she heard actually a distant cackle? She reached deep down inside and ignited her personal fountain of energy. Light filled her body and overflowed, spilling into the room and then raced outward. She let her mind follow one of the brilliant streams of energy.

Glancing back, she saw her house and then her neighborhood growing smaller in the distance. Henrietta could still feel her body lying on the bed in her room, and felt herself taking a deep breath.

Her consciousness rose high into the atmosphere and took a corresponding breath, not a physical one, but an emotionally charged, heavenly breath.

She eventually smiled, but not because she had vanquished some dark force, real or imagined. She grinned because she finally understood something.

A new awareness had set her free. Henrietta H. House knew for certain that the *doubts and fears*–whatever their source within or outside of her–were her biggest enemies. In the end, if she became ruled by them, they would cripple her, making her afraid to do anything at all.

Soaring ever higher, with growing understanding, Henrietta gazed back at earth far below. She wanted to cradle and protect it, and felt a tinge of sadness, being separated so far from something she cared so much about.

After a short time, however, she turned away from the green-blue sphere and let energy build even stronger in her body lying way down there inside the microscopic house that was no longer visible. She willed her energy to expand more fully, and then flow into the vastness of the universe.

As it did so, her awareness accompanied the streaks of light. Mentally glancing backward for a split-second she watched as the earth grew small and vanished.

Another realization struck her then. It was time at last for Henrietta to be the person she was really meant to be. Not a black witch. Not a white witch. Not even simply a good person.

Henrietta H. House had become a power in the universe.

But she was not alone. So were countless others, and underneath it all, she felt a mighty presence. A positive feeling even stronger than love filled her. She reflected back to all those souls struggling on earth. They were just like her. They were all forces in the universe—even Allie and Janna—if they would only realize it. When would they wake up?

When would they let go of pettiness and discover their true identities, release their fears, and take charge of their lives? When would they soar like the mighty eagles they were, and join with her to transform the earth?

Points of color and light formed exquisite patterns in the vast blackness of space, while an amazing celestial symphony played in the background. There were so many new realms to visit.

Henrietta whispered her secret out into the ethereal "winds" of the cosmos. But would anyone hear it?

Back on earth, Henrietta's body stirred. She sat up and looked around. The amulet was clutched in her hand. She lifted it closer to her face and studied the surface. At the end of the line where the tiny star had become a radiant, white-witch-girl, she now shined more brightly than any who had come before her. And in a blast of pure light—Henrietta went supernova.

Glorious illumination filled the bed chamber. The source was definitely not the talisman. It was Henrietta and she basked in that radiance for some time, until things finally became more normal. That is when she noticed something else.

Her room seemed smaller, and not so much like a sanctuary. It was more like a confining space. Even then, it was her special point in the world. Her life had meaning and she was grateful that she had opposed the coven and never completely given up hope. She had prevailed and now she would thrive.

In addition to her new awareness of herself and her surroundings, Henrietta smelled a sweet aroma nearby. Her eyes followed the scent to the top of her dresser.

Brownies! A whole plate of them. Her mouth watered at the thought of eating one. Her mom must have tiptoed in while Henrietta was "asleep."

Smiling once again, Henrietta H. House was home–but not just because she was alone in her room in her family's long-time residence in Monmouth. She now felt at home anywhere in the universe.

That included her town, with all her new friends. Even if they had a lot to learn—and who didn't? She had faith in them, because she had faith in herself.

Henrietta also realized she had one of the most important things any girl could have. For the first time in her life, she had a mother who really cared about her.

Henrietta Hattie House sighed deeply with contentment. Then she crossed over to the dresser and put an entire brownie into her mouth. Her friends had no idea what they were missing out on.

"Ummm!"

ABOUT THE AUTHOR

Born in the wilds of Borneo in the early 1500s, he fought pirates around the world before discovering the fountain of youth that Ponce de Leon was unable to locate. Never satisfied with remaining in one place for long, he wrestled alligators in Australia before going on walkabout for twenty years. He crossed the Alps with Hannibal and sided with the Navateans against Alexander the Great. He never forgave Napoleon for defacing the Sphinx in Egypt—and what a waste of ammunition. He was a wagon train scout along the Oregon trail, after sitting through the horrid Salem Witch Trials and trying to save as many of those poor souls as he could. His early training in magic began in Delphi, directly from the oracles there. He was able to do all of the aforementioned once he uncovered the fabled time machine described by HG Wells. He also started the famous tourist attraction, Bundy's Believe It Or Else, which was predicated on the notion that fiction is truly stranger than fact. His most famous quote to date: "It is all about imagination."

For an abbreviated and slightly different version, see below, and then visit the website:

EA Bundy is an Oregon author who loves to write, travel and read good stories. To learn more about him and the novels he has written or is working on, please visit his website at:
www.eabundyauthor.com